Converted

Revamped Series, Volume 3

W.J. May

Published by Wanita May, 2020.

This is a work of fiction. Similarities to real people, places, or events are entirely coincidental.

CONVERTED

First edition. September 17, 2020.

Written by W.J. May.

Also by W.J. May

Bit-Lit Series
Lost Vampire
Cost of Blood
Price of Death

Blood Red Series
Courage Runs Red
The Night Watch
Marked by Courage
Forever Night
The Other Side of Fear
Blood Red Box Set Books #1-5

Daughters of Darkness: Victoria's Journey
Victoria
Huntress
Coveted (A Vampire & Paranormal Romance)
Twisted
Daughter of Darkness - Victoria - Box Set

Great Temptation Series
The Devil's Footsteps
Heaven's Command
Mortals Surrender

Hidden Secrets Saga
Seventh Mark - Part 1
Seventh Mark - Part 2
Marked By Destiny
Compelled
Fate's Intervention
Chosen Three
The Hidden Secrets Saga: The Complete Series

Kerrigan Chronicles
Stopping Time
A Passage of Time
Ticking Clock
Secrets in Time
Time in the City
Ultimate Future

Mending Magic Series
Lost Souls
Illusion of Power
Challenging the Dark

Castle of Power
Limits of Magic
Protectors of Light

Omega Queen Series
Discipline
Bravery
Courage
Conquer
Strength
Validation

Paranormal Huntress Series
Never Look Back
Coven Master
Alpha's Permission
Blood Bonding
Oracle of Nightmares
Shadows in the Night
Paranormal Huntress BOX SET

Prophecy Series
Only the Beginning
White Winter
Secrets of Destiny

Revamped Series
Hidden
Banished
Converted

Royal Factions
The Price For Peace
The Cost for Surviving
The Punishment For Deception

The Chronicles of Kerrigan
Rae of Hope
Dark Nebula
House of Cards
Royal Tea
Under Fire
End in Sight
Hidden Darkness
Twisted Together
Mark of Fate
Strength & Power
Last One Standing
Rae of Light
The Chronicles of Kerrigan Box Set Books # 1 - 6

The Chronicles of Kerrigan: Gabriel

Living in the Past
Present For Today
Staring at the Future

The Chronicles of Kerrigan Prequel
Christmas Before the Magic
Question the Darkness
Into the Darkness
Fight the Darkness
Alone in the Darkness
Lost in Darkness
The Chronicles of Kerrigan Prequel Series Books #1-3

The Chronicles of Kerrigan Sequel
A Matter of Time
Time Piece
Second Chance
Glitch in Time
Our Time
Precious Time

The Hidden Secrets Saga
Seventh Mark (part 1 & 2)

The Kerrigan Kids
School of Potential

Myths & Magic
Kith & Kin
Playing With Power
Line of Ancestry
Descent of Hope
Illusion of Shadows

The Queen's Alpha Series
Eternal
Everlasting
Unceasing
Evermore
Forever
Boundless
Prophecy
Protected
Foretelling
Revelation
Betrayal
Resolved
The Queen's Alpha Box Set

The Senseless Series
Radium Halos - Part 1
Radium Halos - Part 2
Nonsense
Perception
The Senseless - Box Set Books #1-4

Standalone
Shadow of Doubt (Part 1 & 2)
Five Shades of Fantasy
Zwarte Nevel
Shadow of Doubt - Part 1
Shadow of Doubt - Part 2
Four and a Half Shades of Fantasy
Dream Fighter
What Creeps in the Night
Forest of the Forbidden
Arcane Forest: A Fantasy Anthology
The First Fantasy Box Set

Watch for more at www.wjmaybooks.com.

CONVERTED

REVAMPED SERIES BOOK 1

USA TODAY BESTSELLING AUTHOR

W.J. MAY

Copyright 2020 by W.J. May

THIS E-BOOK OR PRINT is licensed for your personal enjoyment only. This e-book/paperback may not be re-sold or given away to other people. If you would like to share this book with another person, please purchase an additional copy for each recipient. If you're reading this book and did not purchase it, or it was not purchased for your use only, then please return to Smashwords.com and purchase your own copy. Thank you for respecting the hard work of the author.

Have You Read the Hidden Secrets Saga?

Book I – *Seventh Mark Part 1 is free!*

USA TODAY BESTSELLING author, W.J. May brings you a twisted Red Riding Hood fairy-tale that'll get your heart thumping - for fear and love.

Beautiful Rouge has little knowledge about her past, she has questions but has never tried to find the answers. Everything changes when she befriends a strangely intoxicating family. Siblings Grace and Michael, appear to have secrets which seem somehow connected to Rouge. Forced to be apart, Michael and Rouge's worlds collide when a hidden terror threatens to destroy Michael's family. Rouge may be the only one who can find the answer.

An ancient journal, a Sioghra necklace and a special mark force life-altering decisions for a girl who grew up unprepared to fight for her life or others.

All secrets have a cost and Rouge's determination to find the truth may force her and Michael apart. It can only lead to trouble...or something even more sinister.

Warning: There are werewolves in this story... and they are not friendly.

Hidden Secrets Saga:
Seventh Mark - Part 1
Seventh Mark - Part 2
Marked by Destiny
Compelled
Fate's Intervention
Chosen Three
Spin off:
Prophecy Series:
Only the Beginning

White Winter
Secrets of Destiny

Find W.J. May

Website:
https://www.wjmaybooks.com
Facebook:
https://www.facebook.com/pages/Author-WJ-May-FAN-PAGE/
141170442608149
Newsletter:
SIGN UP FOR W.J. May's Newsletter to find out about new releases,
updates, cover reveals and even freebies!
http://eepurl.com/97aYf

Concerted Blurb:

In a future where leadership demands blood, can two outcasts lead their people to a brighter tomorrow?

Tabitha Maslov is the Archon of a besieged Brooklyn.

Staking the former Archon Jeremiah may have handed Tabitha Maslov the reins of power, but that doesn't mean others are willing to accept her leadership. Her motion to shut down the machines pumping pollutants into the sky and end forced donations to the blood banks have other Elders on edge. Members of Jeremiah's former council flout her orders, the Archon Bethania of Manhattan slanders her at every turn, and a rumor spreads through the city that she has awakened the wrath of an ancient Elder council. An unlikely ally offers aid, but even that may not be enough to stop what Tay has set in motion.

With a killer on the loose in Brooklyn, Tay races to find answers about the secretive cabal of vampires that has set its sights on her district. But the cost of saving her city may be higher than she's willing to pay.

Kaiden Ottaker is the Alpha of a divided pack.

He killed Lubok and laid claim to the packs of the East Coast, but Kaiden has been an outcast for a long time. At the Great Eastern Gathering he struggles to unite Shifters who don't trust him. And when a puma comes from the west to offer him a challenge that will legitimize him as Alpha, he has no choice but to take it. But the road to the lost shrine of Shifter legend is long, and the dangers are many. As the journey takes its toll, Kaiden begins to fear that he will never return to New York City.

Down in the depths of an ancient Tomb Kaiden encounters a power he never imagined, and finds himself embroiled in a fight for his life that he isn't sure he can survive.

With their own people turning against them, can Tay and Kaiden face the trials ahead? Or will the backlash against their attempts at change be the end of them both?

Chapter 1

–from a fragment of poetry by an unknown author (BANNED)

In the aftermath of chaos, there is a moment of quiet. A time, however brief, when the whirling momentum must slow and the world's rhythm reasserts itself.

Tabitha Maslov was still waiting for that moment.

Manhattan was a smoldering ruin. Brooklyn, though it had escaped the worst of the fighting, had more than a few bodies in its streets. Worse, though, was the almost certain promise of further conflict to come. Jeremiah was dead and gone, but Bethania, Tay thought, would be a worse enemy, and she didn't just have herself and Kaiden to look out for anymore.

"What are we going to do?" she asked the man beside her.

Kaiden, his dark hair ruffled by the cool breeze that blew over the rooftop, sighed. "Run away?" he suggested, in a tone that said he didn't really consider it a serious proposition.

He'd offered that once before, down in the tunnels below Manhattan. Tay wished, not for the first time, that she had taken him up on it. They could be far away from New York City, making a life for themselves out in the wild places under the stars. Back then, no one would have cared enough to hunt them beyond the boundaries of the city.

It was no use lingering on what might have been, though. That beautiful, impossible dream was forever beyond her reach. The new head of Brooklyn's Elder society couldn't just vanish into the wilderness, and Kaiden had his own weight of responsibility to carry.

"Don't think I haven't thought about it," she said, trying to make the words sound like a joke instead of a desperate desire. "It's a little late for that, though, I think."

Kaiden looked down at the white-suited Servitors hauling bodies out of the compound's main yard. Huddled together against one side of the fence was a small group of Shifters, warily watching the same thing. "Not so sure they'd just let the new Archon of Brooklyn go haring off on a whim," he agreed. He shook his head. "That's still such a strange thing to shape my mouth around. 'Archon Tay.'"

"Archon *Tabitha Maslov*," Tay corrected, deliberately haughty.

"Oh. Of course. How could I possibly have dared such disrespect?" Kaiden flashed her a warm smile that made her heart do a funny little flip in her chest.

Despite all the worry weighing her down, Tay giggled. "Well, I think *Alpha* Kaiden Ottaker of the East Coast has earned a little familiarity."

"Have I?" Abruptly, all of the teasing was gone from Kaiden's voice. He turned to look at her, his eyes startlingly green even in the low light.

Like a piece of forest in all the gray of the city, Tay thought. *He carries the wild places with him.*

"Have you?" she asked, buying time while her heart beat a rapid staccato against her ribs.

"Earned familiarity," Kaiden said, voice low.

He had saved her life, twice. They had made it through the tunnels together, fought their way to Bethania's sanctuary, stopped Lubok's plot. Kaiden had *fed* from her. And in all that time, there had never been even a moment to examine the warmth that flushed through her when she heard his voice.

It was a terrible idea. Even considering it—this thing between them—was insane. But looking into those green eyes, Tay felt all of her objections falling away.

If someone had told her even two weeks earlier that she would be cast out by her Archon and claw her way back to be the primary power in Brooklyn, she would have told them they were losing their mind. But here she was, standing on the roof of the former Archon Jeremiah's sanctuary, watching *her* Servitors clean up the remains of the battle that had won Kaiden his position as dominant Alpha on the East Coast. Over their heads the heavy cloud cover that had insulated the city for almost a decade was fading in patches, and here and there a star glimmered dimly in the dark.

What was one more impossible thing?

Have I earned familiarity? he'd asked. He was still waiting for her answer, his eyes on her face. If she said no he would walk away and never ask again, that she was sure of.

"You've earned more than that," Tay said very softly.

Kaiden's hand lifted slowly, so slowly she could easily have stopped it. The backs of his knuckles tenderly brushed a loose lock of dark hair back from her cheek. Tay trembled under the touch, but not with fear.

"Tay..." The single word was gentle, though his voice was rough with withheld emotion.

"Kiss me," Tay said. "Please."

She didn't want to think any more about whether what they were doing was right or not. She just wanted to wrap herself up in his warmth and never let go.

The hand that had brushed her hair from her cheek curled around the back of her neck, cradling her, and Kaiden bent to press his lips to hers.

Her senses were overwhelmed with the press of his body against hers, the pine and leather scent of him. She wrapped her arms over his broad shoulders and arched in closer. His free hand curled around her hip, large and startlingly warm against the chill of her own body. She sank into him and forgot everything else. Nothing mattered but Kaiden. All she knew, and all she wanted, was him.

Somewhere close, someone cleared his throat.

Tay startled, pulling back from Kaiden, and turned to see Matthias standing in the doorway. She was glad she couldn't blush. Glad, too, that it had been the old Servitor and not someone more likely to take violent issue with finding them together.

"Matthias," she said a little breathlessly. "Did you need something?"

If Matthias had any problem with what he'd seen, he didn't say so. In fact, Tay was quite sure that he was *amused* by what he'd walked in on. Kaiden, who had tensed beside her, seemed to come to the same conclusion, his posture softening.

"The former Archon Jeremiah's counselors are prepared to meet with you, Master," Matthias said, and there was definitely a spark of laughter in his dark eyes, though he didn't let it show in his face. "Though if you are busy..."

How was it he managed to make a jab at her sound so completely respectful? "What have I told you about calling me 'Master'?" Tay sighed. "Please just call me Tay, Matthias. Or Archon if you really have to use a title. Master is just so..."

"Stuck up?" Kaiden suggested. "Jeremiah-ish?"

Tay laughed. "I'm pretty sure it's an Archon thing in general, but yes. I don't want to be associated with Jeremiah at all if I can help it."

"Archon Tabitha, then," Matthias said, acquiescing. "The remains of the former Archon's council await your presence."

Tay sighed. She wanted nothing more than to stay up on the roof with Kaiden, looking out toward the distant hills and forests, making impossible plans to leave it all behind. But an Archon had duties, and hers were just beginning.

She turned, looking one last time at Kaiden over her shoulder, and followed Matthias down the stairs.

Chapter 2

"Trust is a rare commodity in Elder society. Rare and valuable. In a society where most would sacrifice anything or anyone to reach the top of the power structure, such a thing is dearly earned and easily broken."
–from the journals of Nathaniel Lane (BANNED)

Tay was, of course, well-acquainted with the hand-picked faction of Jeremiah's brood who had been closest to him before his death. She had been one of them once, in the early days of her new existence, when she still reveled in the strength the virus granted her. Before she had realized the truth about the Elders and that Jeremiah was the worst of them. She was surprised to learn, though, when she stepped into the room that Matthias indicated, just how few of them were left.

Only three vampires—fewer than a third of those that had once been Jeremiah's inner circle—waited for her. These were the sad remnants of a once-proud group. Calling them Jeremiah's council was, of course, laughable; Jeremiah had never listened to anyone's council but his own. But they had been high up in the hierarchy, the recipients of all of the best Brooklyn had to offer. And here they were, a ragtag bunch of weary survivors, waiting for a near-fledgling half their age to decide their fate.

"Archon Tabitha." Robert, narrow and fidgety and dressed like he'd just walked out of his job at an accounting firm, stepped forward and bobbed his head in a nervous, respectful little bow. "Thank you for agreeing to see us."

"Of course." Tay pulled on a pleasant smile, not believing a bit of the over-exaggerated anxious nerd act. She had seen Robert snap the neck of a Servitor once, cold as ice, over a minor mistake in a calculation. Jeremiah didn't recruit people who weren't willing to kill at the slightest provocation.

Except, apparently, for me. Though he had been proven wrong on that, too, in the end. Had it shocked him, she wondered, that she hadn't hesitated to put a stake in his heart?

Her gaze flicked to the other two: Frederico, a square-jawed first-generation New York Italian who might have been good-looking if he didn't always look so disgustingly smug, and Anya. *Of all the ones who could have survived, did it have to be her?* Tay offered them both the same fake smile she'd given Robert and took a seat, gesturing for them to follow suit.

She and Anya had never gotten along particularly well. The red-haired fledgling, with her big blue eyes and deceptively sweet face, was the only vampire in the room younger than Tay. *She looks like she should be milking cows in an alpine meadow somewhere,* Tay thought a bit uncharitably. Anya had been her replacement when she first fell out of Jeremiah's favor, a handful of years before the events that had ended in her being cast out, and Tay had always found her unbearably certain of her own superiority.

Now, though, Anya looked anything but superior. Her flawless, milk-pale skin was marred with a set of still-healing gouges that ran from the bridge of her nose to the neckline of her high-collared shirt. The souvenir of a Shifter-Lych attack, if Tay had to guess. She would heal eventually, of course; Tay doubted there would even be a scar. But there was a new and fearful unease in her eyes that Tay didn't think would be so easy to shake.

"So," she said, folding her hands on the tabletop in front of her to keep herself from fidgeting. "You are all that remains of the former Archon's hand-picked elite."

"Bet that really makes you happy, doesn't it?" Frederico scoffed, meeting her eyes squarely with his chin lifted and jutting mulishly forward. "Getting your own back? Right, *Archon* Maslov?"

"Killing Jeremiah was 'getting my own back,'" Tay said evenly. "That had nothing to do with the rest of you, or how many of you died. He was the one who created and released the hybrids. He was the one who started the attack on Manhattan and the siege of Archon Bethania's sanctuary that got most of your friends killed. If you want to blame someone, Frederico, blame the person responsible."

"Archon… *Former* Archon Jeremiah was never really known for his self-restraint," Robert offered. "We all knew his rule would end in violence."

Still trying to get in my good graces, Tay thought sourly. But his obsequious manner didn't make him any less right, and everyone in the room knew it.

"What matters now isn't how the Archonate was transferred to new hands," she said. "What matters is dealing with the aftermath of that transition. The three of you were among Jeremiah's most trusted inner circle. That probably means, honestly, that I shouldn't allow you anywhere near this sanctuary or my ear, but I've seen firsthand what casting someone aside can make them." *And they do say keep your enemies closer.* "So I'm willing to give you a chance to prove you're not going to spend the next decade trying to undermine my authority here."

Robert and Anya exchanged a glance. It was difficult to read what the other woman was thinking through the ragged, scabbed-over gouges obscuring her expression, but Tay thought she caught a flicker of uncertainty there.

Frederico crossed his arms over his broad chest. "If you were any kind of smart, you'd kill us and be done with it."

Tay's eyebrows lifted. "Are you telling me that's what you want?"

"I'm telling you it's what any Archon with any bloody sense and the guts to actually run a city would do," Frederico said, like he didn't care that he might be signing his own death warrant. "You stake the Archon, you execute any of his inner circle that didn't defect with you, and you start over with a clean slate." He shrugged. "That's just how it works."

"Things are going to work differently now," Tay said, her tone hard. She wished, fiercely, that Kaiden was sitting next to her. He'd be able to shut Frederico down with a look. But it was best for her to address Jeremiah's people herself, without the added handicap of a hybrid at her side. It didn't mean she didn't miss his steady strength, the warm, *living* scent of him, the sense of a guardian at her side.

For a moment, her mind flashed back to the rooftop, to Kaiden's arms around her and his mouth on hers. In fifty years, nothing had made her feel alive like Kaiden's kiss did. When this endless, awful meeting was over, maybe—

"Define 'differently,'" Anya said, speaking for the first time. Her usually-smooth voice was rough, and Tay wondered just how much damage the collar of her shirt hid.

Tay took a deep breath. Everything else had been precursor to what she was about to say. This was the moment their conversation had been leading up to, and she didn't think they were going to like it. "To start with, no more culls. The former Archon's obsession with insurgents and the plots he constantly believed were going on around him only served to create unrest in the city and discontent among the mortals."

"And what do you plan to do about the Shifter problem?" Robert asked.

"Nothing," Tay said. "I meant what I said last night. Brooklyn will be a haven for all species: Elders, Shifters, mortals. We're done with the fighting and the forced blood donation, hunting humans in the streets, all of it. We're going to create a place where everyone can live in harmony."

All three of them stared at her.

"Are you out of your freakin' mind?" Frederico sputtered after a moment of appalled silence. "You want us to make nice with those animals?" He flung out a hand toward the woman sitting next to him. "Look what they did to Anya, for night's sake."

Matthias, standing behind Tay's chair, cleared his throat disapprovingly.

"The Shifters are under new leadership," Tay said, keeping her voice even with some effort. "And they have agreed to a truce."

"And you believe that crap?"

"It does seem... ill-advised," Robert said more cautiously. "It's certainly unprecedented. Are you sure now is the best time, what with the fact that we should be preparing for, at the very least, an attack from Manhattan in the near future? Archon Winterbourne in Staten Island is likely to accept your ascension, but there's no telling how Queens will react. It's entirely possible than Archon Zyanya will join the Archon Bethania in her move against us."

"In which case we want the Shifters on our side." Tay stared them all down. "Jeremiah won Manhattan and lost Brooklyn in the same night because he was fighting a two-front war. I'm not going to make the same mistake."

Whatever else Robert was, no one had ever been able to call him stupid. He nodded slowly, wheels turning behind his eyes, and Tay knew he was at least considering what she had to say.

"Anya?" she prompted, her gaze moving to the redhead. "What are your thoughts?"

If Anya was surprised to be asked, she didn't show it. Her head tipped thoughtfully to one side. "Honestly? I know you and I haven't exactly seen eye to eye in the past, Archon, but... Jeremiah was losing it those last few months. We all saw it. The culls. Naming whole broods Feral. The creation of those beasts he unleashed on Manhattan." She shook her head. "I don't know if your way is any less insane, but maybe it's better."

Tay had to consciously stop her mouth from dropping open. *Am I really getting support from* Anya?

"You're kidding, right?" Frederico, apparently as shocked as Tay was, slammed a hand down on the table. "You can't tell me you're actually supporting this touchy-feely pipe dream!"

"Think about it, Freddy," Anya said, trying to pacify him. "We lost a lot of people in Manhattan, and a lot of the Servitors when the Shifters hit. We're not going to be prepared to stand against Manhattan without some help, especially if Archon Bethania manages to talk Queens over to her side. This might be the best chance we have."

"No. No way!" Frederico stood up so fast his chair tipped back on two legs. "You're absolutely losing your marbles on this, every last one of you! And I'm not going to sit around and play along!"

"You walk out of this room and that's it," Tay said. She rose, more calmly than he had. "You'll be stripped of your status as council member, and all privileges and rank you might once have held will be gone, your place in this sanctuary included. So you had better be sure."

He met her eyes, his own dark and furious. Tay half-expected to watch fangs slide into place over his canines.

"Freddy," Anya said.

"Think about this," Robert added.

Frederico laughed sharply. "I've already thought about it. You two suck-ups want to stay here and bow to the new order, you go right ahead. But I'm not gonna sit around and watch this jumped-up Blood Doll ruin everything our Archon built."

"Fine," Tay bit out. "Matthias, please see to it that Frederico is escorted out of the sanctuary and that the guards know not to readmit him."

"Of course, Archon." Matthias gave a little bow and opened the door.

Frederico looked them all over one more time, lip curling into a sneer, and then stormed out. Matthias followed silently behind. The door clicked shut.

"He's going to be trouble later," Robert said.

"Then he'll be dealt with," Tay answered. But she couldn't help thinking, as she listened to the sound of his footsteps recede down the hall, that maybe she should have just taken his original advice and disposed of him entirely.

Chapter 3

"Love is the only true freedom left to us."
–mortal saying

"What if I'm making the wrong choice?" Tay paced the length of the room she'd given Kaiden, and then spun on her heel and stalked back again. The space wasn't particularly small, but she made it feel like a cage, and it was setting the beast inside Kaiden on edge. "Maybe Frederico is right. All of this is completely insane. No one has ever done anything like it before, and I doubt they're going to let me get away with it now."

Kaiden had never met the Elder Tay was referring to, but he knew enough about Jeremiah to take a guess at what kind of person he would be. "Frederico is a power-hungry bully, too caught up in his own self-interest to wrap his mind around the idea that anyone could ever do anything just because it was the right thing to do."

Tay laughed, short and sharp. "That sounds about right," she admitted, slowing her steps to turn and look at Kaiden. "But *is* it the right thing to do? I mean, what makes us think that we have the right to dismantle an entire society? And that's assuming we're even capable of it." Her shoulders slumped, her expression sliding into worry. "What can two people do against a system that's been in place for decades?"

Kaiden rose from his place at the end of the neatly-made bed and wrapped his arms around her, drawing her in close against his chest. She sighed and sank into the embrace, letting his strength hold her upright. They'd barely had space to breathe since he'd rescued her from Lubok's agents, and neither of them was likely to get much R&R any time soon. But as much as he wanted to just wrap Tay in his arms and hide from the world with her, they both had responsibilities they couldn't ignore.

"We may be just two people," he said, "but we've been given access to a kind of power that most in the Predatory Society spend their lifetimes trying to achieve and never reach. We have the leverage to move the world, as long as we apply it properly."

"And how do we do that?" Tay asked against his chest.

"Slow and steady," Kaiden said. "We can't change the world in a day. We have to get people on our side, supporters who will back us when we make our move."

"Who's going to support the destruction of their entire way of life?"

"It's our way of life, too," Kaiden pointed out. "Or it was. And we're prepared to work against it. There have to be others like us, people who recognize that this is unsustainable, that we share more commonalities with the mortals than not. Our position gives us the opportunity and the vantage point to seek them out."

Tay sighed, long and shuddering. "You're right," she admitted. "I know you are. I'm just..."

"Scared?" Kaiden chuckled without much mirth. "Me, too. I'm terrified."

Her head lifted, her dark eyes searching his expression. Even with the weight of recent events on his shoulders, Kaiden found himself caught in their depths. It still astonished him, the way that he fell for her anew every time they had a moment of peace between them. She was a vampire, a creature born of the virus that he so despised in himself. He should have despised her just as deeply. But looking into her eyes, all he wanted was to be by her side for as long as possible.

Which made the news he had to give her all the more difficult.

"I know this is a lot," he said, savoring the sensation of her slender frame wrapped in his arms for as long as he could. "It seems impossible.

But we've already done the impossible. You were Feral. I was cast out by my own people. And now we're in a position to make a real difference."

Tay smiled. It was a small, hesitant thing, but it still made him feel warm in a way that nothing else had for a long time. "From Feral to Archon," she said thoughtfully. "I would never have been able to do it without you."

"You saved my life," Kaiden said. "Everything we achieved, we achieved together."

Before he had time to say anything more, Tay pushed up on her toes and kissed him. Kaiden's arms tightened around her, pulling her in closer.

They'd had so little time together. The world seemed determined to pull them apart at every turn. And he was going to have to tell Tay in a moment that it was about to do so yet again. But first he wanted a chance to just hold her. To feel her lips against his. He breathed in the familiar scent of her and gave himself up to the kiss.

When they pulled apart Kaiden was breathless, his senses overwhelmed with the nearness of Tay. He could have gone on like that, knowing nothing but her, but he was already cutting it close. He pulled back enough to look into her eyes.

"Tay..." He sighed. "I'm going to have to leave the city."

Her eyebrows drew together, her hands gripping his upper arms. "What?"

"I'm the Alpha of a Shifter pack..." Kaiden watched understanding settle in her expression and offered her a smile he didn't really feel.

"You have to go where the Shifters are. Of course." Tay shook her head. "I should have realized. I was just so caught up in everything else that I didn't stop to think about it." Her voice was bleak.

"I'm sorry, Tay." Kaiden drew her close again, wishing he didn't have to ever let her go. "I wouldn't leave you if there was any way I could avoid it."

"I know." She lay her head against his shoulder with a quiet sigh. "I just wish... I wish that we could manage to go more than a day at a time before we have to split up again."

Kaiden didn't point out that she'd left him the first time. It didn't seem like the moment for it, and he'd long since forgiven her for that. She'd been afraid and alone, still used to a world where no one could be trusted.

"So do I," he told her. He'd never wanted anything more. "And I'll be back just as soon as I can, I promise."

"How far do you have to go?"

"About a day outside of the city," Kaiden told her. He slipped a hand under her chin, gently guiding her head up so that he could kiss her again, long and slow.

Tay sank into it, her body melting against his. Time ceased to have meaning. All he could think of was her. He gave himself over to it, knowing that soon he would have to leave her. But not just yet. They had a little while longer yet, and he intended to make the most of what time they had.

Chapter 4

"The Duties of the Archon: to tend their flock, to defend their District, to cultivate blood."
—To Rule the Undying: Second Mandate

*A*nyone who wants control over an entire District is clearly mad, Tay thought, resisting the urge to reach up and rub her temples. The headache was more imagined than real, a leftover memory of her mortal days. But that didn't dampen the desire to soothe it. *Why did I ever think this was a good idea?*

She looked up at the line of monitors on the wall and sighed. One view of Brooklyn after another stretched across them, but the one she looked at—the one she wanted to escape into—held the feed from the drone camera permanently pointed westward. Toward the Pennsylvania mountains and the woods Kaiden had disappeared into nearly two weeks before.

Tay sent her thoughts arrowing out into that dark stretch of landscape. Somewhere far beyond the reach of the city lights, under a sky full of stars, Kaiden was attempting to sway the Shifter packs to his side.

Since the Battle for the Boroughs (as it was beginning to be called), an uneasy silence had reigned over the city. In Manhattan and The Bronx, Bethania was consolidating her control. Queens and Staten Island watched and waited. And at home in Brooklyn, Elders, mortals, and Shifters were settling into a tentative truce—each of them attempting to work out where they stood in the new pecking order.

In the days that followed her meeting with the remainder of Jeremiah's brood, Tay had dismantled the atmospheric engines that had once pumped smog out over her Archonate. Ongoing efforts in the other four boroughs, and the size of New York City, kept them from achieving a clear sky over Brooklyn. Nevertheless, the heavy cloud cover had dissipated and here and there the stars were visible. It was a boon for the vast majority of the population and, thus far, not particularly popular with the portion of it that had once been the ruling elite.

Not that I'm particularly shocked by their displeasure, Tay thought ruefully. Why would any of them want to see the climate program ended, when its results had put their assumed enemies at a disadvantage and allowed them the run of the dusk and dawn? Still, to her surprise, a small handful of Brooklyn's Elders had stood behind her in her decision. No more than a couple dozen, but even that was a larger number than she had expected. It was a surprise for which she had, undoubtedly, Anya and Robert to thank.

Robert's assistance in the matter was less astonishing. He knew his best chances were with the new regime. Jeremiah, and consequently his closest companions, had never been particularly popular with the other Archons; trying his luck in Staten Island or Queens would end in a considerable downgrade of his status. And as for the other two boroughs...

Bethania could not openly encourage defectors from Tay's Archonate to join her supporters without earning the ire of other watching Archons—not only in New York City, but up and down the eastern seaboard. But that didn't mean she wasn't doing it covertly. More than a few of those most opposed to the new policies in Brooklyn had turned up later in Manhattan or The Bronx. Robert, though, had been closer than most to the man who had burned down much of Bethania's District and killed nearly a third of her population. He wasn't likely to receive a particularly warm welcome. Tay wasn't surprised by that.

No. It was Anya whose response bewildered her. Because Anya, to all appearances, had actually come over to Tay's side.

The dream that Tay shared with Kaiden, of a city where no one race dominated over the others, meant the end of Elder rule. The end of the Predatory Society itself. It would be a new order, based not on greed and hunger and 'might makes right' but instead on the needs of *all* who lived within Brooklyn's borders. *And perhaps, one day, even beyond.*

It was not a dream she had shared with even her closest Servitor allies, let alone any of the Elders. But even the watered-down version made palatable for public consumption was not something she would have ever expected Anya to accept.

Without the end of the Elders' reign, Kaiden would always be a second-class citizen. Tay loved him, and couldn't stand by and leave that uncontested. But Anya, an Elder whose looks and intelligence could likely gain her a favorable position in any city she chose to settle in, had nothing to gain and everything to lose by supporting Tay's agenda.

So why? Tay wondered, not for the first time. What purpose did it serve her?

What kind of scheme is she devising behind my back?

A heartbeat later, she realized whose voice the thought spoke in. Horrified, Tay shook the suspicion off. She wasn't Jeremiah, to see betrayal and collusion everywhere, and she wasn't going to let becoming an Archon make her into that.

How is she supposed to be plotting to derail a plan she doesn't even know is in motion? Tay reminded herself. All Anya knew was that Tay was shutting down the atmospheric engines for the sake of the mortals, and allowing Shifters into their city in an attempt to strengthen their forces against Bethania.

Unless she's figured it out, the part of her that sounded far too much like Jeremiah for her own comfort whispered. *It's not that big a leap of logic. And if* Anya *knows, then—*

Tay hissed through her teeth, fingers curling around the arms of the chair she sat in. She was being absurd. Anya, like Robert, knew how to cozy up to the powerful, and somehow that had become Tay. That was all it was.

She couldn't let herself give in to paranoia. If she did that, she'd become the very man she had fought so hard to save herself from.

Chapter 5

"Rule with strength or do not rule at all."
–Archon proverb

Tay had decided to move the traditional command center of the Archon of Brooklyn from the location where Jeremiah, her sire, had established it. He had been a proponent of modern technology: drones and radio-controlled gun turrets, and wide-screen monitors running live feeds of news from every corner of The Archonate he controlled. At a word from him, the rattling fingers of his technicians had brought down targeted death on any who opposed him.

For her part Tay could stand the distance of it, like a spider in the middle of its web. She had moved the whole command center to an old hotel, renovating its basements and lower floors to make them light-proof. Matthias had insisted that she also make the place a visually acceptable seat of power for an Archon.

The hall where she currently sat was wood-paneled, with a tiled floor. The screens and feeds sat along one wall opposite the Archon's chair, which Tay had pushed to keep simple. She'd wanted nothing as tall or grand as the previous one, but Chief Servitor Matthias had still made sure that it sat on its own raised platform, and that it was big enough for her to lounge back in, peering down at her 'subjects' like a queen of old.

There was a commotion at the door.

A pair of Servitors in white armor entered, flanking Frederico. Tay wasn't particularly surprised to see him back so soon under guard. She was also not particularly looking forward to dealing with whatever problem he had caused.

It was bound to happen sooner or later. She sighed. *I had hoped it would be later, though.*

"Frederico," Tay said, looking down at the Elder brought before her. "I assume this is not a visit made for pleasure."

"Archon Maslov," the Servitor on the right said, saluting smartly. "The Elder Frederico has drained a human."

"He asked for it," Frederico said, shrugging. He wore a leather jacket and worn jeans.

Tay clutched the chair arms, taking a deep, steadying breath. Of course Frederico had already murdered some hapless mortal. "He *asked* for you to drain him dry?" she asked flatly.

It wasn't completely unheard of for humans to decide on suicide by draining via Elder. For some, like the Blood Dolls, being fed on was a kind of addictive pleasure. But Tay somehow did not think Frederico had been brought in for draining a willing Blood Doll.

He had likely been bored. All of his usual entertainments—rounding up recalcitrant mortals for blood bank donations, joining the groups of Elders that raced through the city hunting suspected insurgents during the culls—had ended with the change in authority. Any privileges he might have earned, any favors he might have been owed, were no longer his. Her Servitors had reported to her that he was living in an apartment block in the north of Brooklyn. It was one of the most expensive a mortal could possible afford, but for an Elder it was a clear sign of disgrace and loss of status.

Yes, Tay could see it. He had been angry, frustrated, at the change of leadership. He had sought to lash out, and decided that the life of the human next door was still worth less than the trouble his actions would cause.

"Elder Frederico," Tay prompted.

"The human in question," the Servitor said, "was the nephew of the Williams family—relatively wealthy importers and exporters. They

claim that he had no history as a Blood Doll and would never have con-
sented to being killed."

"How would they know?" Frederico scoffed.

"They would know better than you, I think," Tay snapped, trying
to keep a rein on her temper. "Are you unaware, Elder Frederico, that
times have completely and utterly changed?"

Frederico's dark eyes met hers in blatant challenge. "I was there for
your whole little speech about human dignity or whatever."

"Then you should be well aware of the fact that the wanton killing
of mortals is strictly outlawed in Brooklyn now," Tay said, meeting his
challenging look with her own. "By what right do you directly disobey
the order of your Archon?"

Frederico's lip curled. "Not *my* Archon," he mumbled under his
breath.

Anger rushed hot through Tay's chest. She rose, fangs sliding into
place, and snarled down at him. "*What* did you say to me?"

"Nothing, my lady." Frederico bowed low. "There must've been
a miscommunication somewhere. There's been so much chaos in the
transition, after all."

Another veiled insult, Tay thought, her hands starting to shake
themselves into claws at her sides. *Keep it together, Tay. Don't lose it in
front of everyone...*

On the steps below her, Frederico was grinning. Tay could see that
this was just what he'd wanted: a chance to challenge her, to make her
look weak in front of her staff and the few other Elders in her service.
He was half a century or more her senior. If he could goad her into a
physical attack he would be within his rights to answer with physical
violence. And if he managed to kill her, he would inherent the Archon's
position. Might made right in the predatory society.

"I forbade it," Tay hissed, drawing herself up to the greater height
afforded her by the stairs she stood on and clamping down on her rage.

If he made his move—attacked her first—her guard would put him down and that would be the end of it.

Do it, she thought viciously. She wouldn't kill him unprovoked.

But he has provoked you, another darker part of herself whispered, too much like the part that had looked at Anya and seen a threat. It was a part of her that knew only violence, that believed rule came by blood and power was held with fang and claw. *His words have already earned him a death sentence!*

Tempting as the idea was, though, Tay knew she couldn't give in to it. Any other Archon in the city would have killed him out of hand for breaking their law. Any other Archon would have never let him live long enough to do it. He'd told her as much, the day after Jeremiah's death, when she'd sat him and his brood mates down to speak with them.

You know exactly where the boundaries are, don't you? She stared down at Frederico's sneer, and so badly wanted to smack it from his face. But if she called the guards to take him down without a viable threat to her life, she would be asking them to make a decision. *Asking them to choose sides: me and the new way, or Frederico and the predatory society. How many of them, if they had the chance to really decide, would side with me over the comfortable, familiar status quo?*

"I'll be sure to remember that in future," Frederico said, in a hall gone suddenly very cold and very still. Tay could feel the eyes of everyone in the room on her—questioning. Judging.

"Elder Frederico." Tay drew in a steadying breath. "You are hereby ordered to pay the blood-sum of one life to the family of the youth you killed. You will pay it, and you will *apologize*."

The glee on Frederico's face died abruptly. In its place was shock. "Apologize?" he blurted before he could stop himself. "Are you kidding me?"

"Yes, *apologize*," Tay retorted. "To Simon's family. Sincerely. And if I hear from them that you have not, or that you have in any way shirked your duty, I'll pronounce you Feral. Understood?"

Feral. That word stung in her ears even as it left her own lips. It was what had started all of this, so long ago. Jeremiah had pronounced *her* Feral, and while on the run she had been saved by Kaiden. From there, the events had followed the bloody path that led to the very steps where she stood. Tay didn't even *like* the idea of Feral vampires, Elders outside the fold of society, unfed and unwanted, growing monstrous. But she had no greater threat against those like Frederico, who would see her thrown down from her place before she ever accomplished those goals she was striving so hard to reach.

"Feral?" Frederico breathed, astonished. "You would do that to me?"

If I exile other Elders, will I, like Jeremiah, just be creating an army of discontents and rebels destined to overthrow me?

Tay took a step closer, showing the audience that she was not afraid of the larger, older vampire. "I would do more than that, Frederico," she said coolly. "I said if you shirk your duty, I will have you exiled. If you directly cross me again, though? I'll kill you with my own hands."

Anger and disbelief followed shock across Frederico's face. It was the answer that he had been pushing for, a direct challenge, but not in the way he'd wanted it. He had wanted an outright attack, a fight he could respond to physically. Instead, she'd given him a choice. Now it was clear he knew the boundaries. In the eyes of those around them, if he stepped outside of them again it would be on his own head. She had turned the tables on him and he knew it.

Would he go racing toward disrespect and doom, Tay wondered, or would he take advice and heed her warning?

The silence stretched between them, tension holding the room in stasis.

"Fine!" he snarled, snapping the brittle quiet. He spun on his heel and stalked out.

"Archon Tabitha?" said a smooth voice beside her. Tay wheeled to see her Chief Servitor, Matthias, his faded umber skin lined with age. "There is a matter to attend to."

"Of course." Tay followed him from the chamber, grateful for the escape from all the watching eyes. Silently, she thanked whatever stars had aligned to ensure that this man was on her side. Matthias had the best political instincts of anyone she had ever met.

They walked through the door at the back of the Archon's Hall, to where a much smaller private chamber sat at the back, furnished in a simple and austere style.

"No word?" Tay asked as soon as the door had closed. This room was the only one in the entire building that was completely soundproof, a 'silent' room for the most private of discussions.

"No, Archon Tabitha," Matthias sighed.

It wouldn't have been hard for him to guess what she was asking about. Since Kaiden had announced there was a tribe-gathering of all the local Shifters, and that he had to attend, it was all that Tay could think about. Was Kaiden safe? How was he getting on? What if the whole thing had been a trap? She must have asked Matthias a dozen times already for news.

Like her, Kaiden had taken over his Alpha position in combat from another whose followers resented both the killing of their original leader and—more vehemently—the fact that Kaiden was a part vampire, part Shifter abomination.

Matthias' even voice cut through Tay's whirling thoughts. "Elder Frederico will be a problem, you know."

"I know," Tay grumbled.

"Jeremiah would have killed him for less," Matthias suggested gently.

"I am *not Archon Jeremiah!*" Tay snarled, teeth bared at the Servitor, who appeared to not even notice her outburst. The human's apparent nonchalance made Tay feel silly and inexperienced, shame knotting in her stomach.

"I'm sorry, Matthias." She rubbed at her temples. "I'm just tired already. One month into the job and I'm tired. How, by the night itself, am I ever going to manage this? How am I possibly the right person to bring this city out of the darkness?"

Matthias was silent for a long moment. "It's a difficult thing, Archon Tabitha... Jeremiah was a terrible ruler, but the Elders could understand him. They knew what he was."

"And they can't understand *me*." Tay looked up sharply. "Is that what you're saying?"

Matthias sighed. "They understand that you killed Jeremiah, and why. They understand that you were a Feral who rose, through blood, over the bodies of your enemies to become Archon. The Elders... If you will forgive me, Archon, for saying so, as a Servitor who has not been chosen to become a full-blooded Elder—" Tay noted the slight accusation in his voice, but made no comment. "—I've had the opportunity to study you at close proximity.

"It seems to me that the Elders I've met don't mind violence, or hierarchy, or even murder. If you're strong enough to take and hold your position, then they will respect that. *That* is why there are those rebels like Frederico who long for the days of Jeremiah. He was a terrible Archon, and a monstrous individual, but he operated by rules that they knew and could navigate. You, with your talk of unifying the races, are something else entirely. And they are not going to come around to your ideals quickly."

"What are you suggesting, Matthias?" Tay demanded.

"I am suggesting that you may need to consolidate your power through a show of strength, if you want to have the leverage in the future to move forward with your plans," Matthias said carefully.

"So you're telling me I should perform my own cull against those Elders like Frederico? That I should kill anyone who opposes me?" Tay shook her head. "I want an *end* to the bloodshed. Not to cause more!"

"I'm not telling you what you should or should not do, Archon Tabitha. I wouldn't presume to." Matthias met her eyes. "I am simply telling you that those rebels would understand your actions."

"They would do more than understand it; they expect it, Matthias!" Tay huffed, exasperated. "They're trying to trap me. If I round up all of those still loyal to Jeremiah's policies, I'll plunge Brooklyn into another war. One we certainly can't afford right now. With Archon Bethania in both Manhattan and the Bronx, it's only a matter of time before the rebels seek her aid in deposing me. And I'll not give them the excuse!"

"Yes. I had rather thought that was their plan as well," Matthias said evenly. "But how can you deal with enemies inside your District as well as at the borders?"

The Shifters. Tay didn't say anything, just looked at her hands. *If Kaiden can unify the tribes at the Gathering, then he can bolster our defenses with warriors from among them while I deal with rebels and malcontents like Frederico.*

"You know me, Matthias. I always find a way... *somehow.*" Tay tried to find conviction, but the words fell flat. With every day that Kaiden was gone, her hope grew dimmer. What was she going to do if he never returned at all?

Chapter 6

"There appear to be three great Tribes of Shifter clans in North America: the Eastern Tribe (fierce, sparse, nearly extinct) made up of nearly five different clan packs. The Middle Tribe (smaller still, and mostly constrained to the Canadian border and the Great Lakes region), and the Western Tribe (who
have shunned the cities entirely, at least ten clan packs evident)."
–the Helsing Papers (BANNED)

Why would anyone want *to be an Alpha?* Kaiden growled to himself, unaware of the way his thoughts echoed those of the woman he loved many miles away.

His setting and hers, however, could not have been more different. The Archon Tabitha Maslov reclined on a plush and elaborate throne; Kaiden stood on a slab of rock. Where Tay was surrounded by wall screens and video feeds, Kaiden was surrounded by the mixed forests of northern New York state. Where Tay had polished floors, reeking of varnish and resin to her sensitive nose, Kaiden could smell the soft earth and rich mud, the green growing things, and the comings and goings of the many scent trails that crisscrossed the clearing.

One thing was exactly the same, however, and that was the glares on the faces of those who watched them. People who should be loyal to their new leaders, but who instead were only demonstrating malice toward them.

Kaiden stood on the Speaker's Rock, facing down the other leaders, chiefs, and heads of the many packs and tribes that comprised the East Coast Shifter societies. Almost all of them were in their human form (human vocal cords being far more suited to manipulating complex sounds for recognizable speech, and human minds being more suited to the contemplation of complex ideas), but a few had chosen to remain in their completely shifted forms. Scattered about the clearing were a giant timber wolf, a few creatures like hulking and hunched rats, foxes, a couple of bears, and even one mountain lion. Gigantism was one of the genetic defects of the Shifter virus. Mass could not be created from thin air, nor sloughed off and then returned. And so, since in human form they were humans of generally average size, all that body mass had to go somewhere in the shift. So overly large animal forms (and occasionally exceptionally small human forms) were one of the visible signs of a Shifter family. A sign the Elders had too often used in the past to hunt them down.

The other obvious giveaway was the middle shapes of the Shifters: the half-canine, half-human bipedal dog creatures who fought with clawed hands and rending teeth; shaggy humanoid forms with the heads and claws of bears; and so on. These creatures, caught partway between animal and man, were battle forms, and monstrously powerful.

Kaiden's eyes flickered over the members of the Tribes who had chosen to stay in their were-forms—a deliberate and dangerous provocation. They were saying they were ready for a fight, should they need to be. And had the Alpha standing on the Speaker's Rock been anyone but him, such a statement would have been considered terribly bad etiquette. But despite Kaiden's very traditional taking of the mantle of power, tradition had in many other ways fallen to the wayside with his ascension to leadership.

"Filkin?" Kaiden nodded to lean, dark-haired man currently in were-form, a Rat Shifter from a very small tribe that lived in and around the city sewers. He had come with his partner, an older woman wrapped in many layers of clothing and constantly complaining about the scent of pine trees and the forest mud. The Rat family were some of the most urban of all the Shifters, able to hide themselves from the Elders' ravages by descending underground. Most Shifters hated the city, they hated Kaiden's suggestions, and they hated Kaiden himself for being a half-vampire, half-Shifter abomination.

"Thank you, *Chief* Kaiden." Filkin bopped his furred head and Kaiden's lip curled. The emphasis on his title had not been of the respectful sort. "I appreciate your suggestions and, of course, your position now that Chief Lubok is, uh… no longer with us."

Kaiden winced as a number of throaty growls erupted from the back of the crowd. Lubok had been the previous War Chief and Tribe Leader of most of the Shifter packs on the East Coast, and well-respected by many of them. He had also, in Kaiden's opinion, been a brute and a bully, and Kaiden felt no remorse for ending his life.

"However, I have some reservations I must voice," Filkin went on. "You all know that my tribe spends a lot of our time in the city. You all know how close we are to some of the mortals there."

There were nods and murmurs of agreement from the crowd. The Rat family had once been ostracized for their close association with the city mortals, because the city mortals could so easily be dominated by their Elder overlords.

"Whatever you think of us, we are just like the rest of you: we thrive in our natural habitat. The difference is that we are natives to the city. We have contacts and informants, secret ways in and out of the city. We know it, and the people there, better than we know the woods. And what we know is this:

"The City of New York will fall, and before it falls it will burn."

Kaiden stiffened. What gave the Rat Chief the *gall*? By what right did he claim that Archon Tabitha would fall? That Kaiden would fail?

"How can you know that?" Kaiden demanded.

The Rat preened his claws and said in a rasping, not quite human voice, "The Rat family has, as I've said, spent a long time living in the city. We've seen Archons come and go, human vigilantes rise and fall, watched the Shifter War Chiefs throw themselves against the might of the Elders. Do you know how we alone, of all the Shifters, manage not only to survive but to *thrive* in the territory of our worst enemies? We stay out of sight, we watch, and we take advantage of our enemy's weaknesses. This is the way of the Predatory Society."

Filkin sighed, as if it pained him to have to explain this concept to one as high-ranking as Kaiden. "Never has there been such turmoil in the city as there is now. Two of the Archons are dead, their territories handed over to others. And one of those is possibly the most hated Archon in the history of the city. Even more so than her predecessor, and he was *Archon Jeremiah!*"

"Be careful what you say, Rat," Kaiden growled, feeling his ire building, trying to become a rage that would threaten to consume everything.

"It's true!" Filkin pressed on, ignoring Kaiden's fury. "There are usually five Archons to balance and play off each other, to make sure that there are no ties in the vote. Now, though, Archon Tabitha rules a divided District, while Bethania holds both Manhattan and The Bronx and has the backing of more than a few deserters from Brooklyn. And now you want the Shifters involved? There is no good reason for it."

"*I* see good reason!" The voice belonged to Graham Larson, a chief of one of the northernmost packs of Wolf Shifters. Larson's lot held hard to old tradition, much of it harsh and bloody. They were also some of the strongest fighters the East Coast Shifters had. "Any Elder we can remove from the world of the living is an Elder that will trouble us no longer; any weakness might ripple their whole crooked system!"

There was a cheer from some of those around the rock, but Filkin just sneered. "And you, Larson, would burn the city down, too, I bet, on your way out!"

Larson grinned savagely, defiantly, at the Rat. "Like you, we take advantage of opportunity as it comes. The city is a blight on the landscape."

"The city is *our home*!" Filkin hissed, causing others in the crowd to growl.

"Enough!" Kaiden shouted, slamming his booted foot against the rock. Silence fell uneasily over the assembly. "Thank you," Kaiden said, "for your addition, Larson, but I think you misunderstand me. I'm not suggesting that we wipe New York City from the face of the earth. I'm offering us a chance to go *create*, to make a place that is safe for all of us, and not just the Elders."

He turned to Filkin. "Are you telling me, Brother Rat, that your people would not rejoice at the opportunity to walk safely through the streets of Brooklyn?"

Filkin barked a sharp-edged laugh. "Of course we would! But that isn't what you're offering us, Chief Kaiden. Not truly. This pet Archon of yours cannot guarantee the safety of my kind, not until she has consolidated power she can *hold*. Too many oppose her now. You're offering us a future that is many years in the making, if it's anything more than an impossible dream at all!"

"It will never be anything more if we do not take steps toward that future now!" Kaiden insisted.

Anger roiled through the gathered Shifters.

Chapter 7

"A wolf never tires, a rat is never found, but a cat never forgets,"
–Shifter proverb

A snarl ripped through the rising tide of whispers, silencing the assembly. On its heels, a lithe figure stalked into the center of the clearing. She wore denims, a flannel jacket and heavy boots, and carried both a machete and a gun openly on her belt. Her hair was sun-bleached blonde, darker underneath, and her eyes glinted green in the gloom.

An angry harrumph came from the largest figure in the gathering—a hulking Bear-Shifter busy inscribing the minutes of the meeting on long rolls of birch bark paper. The Archivist looked down his snout at the new arrival, annoyed by this interruption of arcane protocol. "Your name, clan, and tribe for the Archive?"

"Maura Tol," she spat. "Central North Tribe. Family of the Puma."

There were a few grumbles and growls from the crowd. The tribes of Shifters on the east coast, though they encompassed many of the major Shifter forms, were canine-heavy, and it was no secret that the Cat-Shifters were as often the targets of their rage as they were their allies.

"What brings a *Cat* to this meeting?" sneered Larson.

"The scent of ignorance," Maura retorted. Larson growled and Maura hissed, and Kaiden leapt down between them.

"If we cannot avoid fighting each other, then how to do any of you expect to fight the Elders?" Kaiden thundered.

"Exactly my point," Maura said delicately. "Thank you for making it for me." She turned to Kaiden, her green eyes brazenly appraising him. "I've never met an Abomination before. You aren't as monstrous as I expected."

Kaiden bit back the urge to snarl at her, fists clenching. "I've never met one of the Puma family either," he said tightly. *Don't let her get to you.* "So you agree that unification is the answer? We come together to fight Archon Bethania?"

"Ha!" Maura barked. "No!"

"You just said—"

"I just said that we shouldn't be fighting amongst ourselves," the Cat-Shifter said, cutting him off. "I said nothing about Archon Bethania."

Her eyes were hard and cold, and Kaiden met them with his own, the silent challenge sparking between them.

"Chief Tol of the Puma?" the Archivist's tone was short and displeased. "What point, exactly, did you come here to raise?"

"This one," Maura Tol said, tearing her eyes from Kaiden's and turning to the rest of the group. "Like all of you, the Puma family received word of a Gathering on the east coast, with the news that the old War Chief had been deposed. Good, I say! Lubok was no friend to us!" she shouted at the crowd, arms raised.

More than a few hackles lifted among the canines.

"But what I've come here to point out is this: Before we embark on another crusade, before we turn on those packs and loners who refuse to take part in still more pointless fighting, hunting them down and treating them like traitors, let us think *Why?* Why did we follow Lubok when he called? Why do we follow this Kaiden now?"

A moment of silence as the gathered assembly parsed her words.

"Lubok," the Cat-Chief continued, "gave us a common enemy. We were united against the Elders. We *needed* a War Chief then, to keep us alive. But—and I say this, Chief Kaiden, with the deepest respect—why do we need one now? Do we need to have another crusade? Are our lives in danger anymore, now that two Archons of the city have died and the Elders fight amongst themselves?"

"They won't fight amongst themselves forever!" Larson snapped.

"Are you suggesting that we all go back to cowering in the forgotten corners of the wild?" Filkin snorted. His black button eyes watched the Cat closely.

Maura turned slowly back to stare Kaiden squarely in the face. "I'm suggesting that we don't need a War Chief anymore."

"Do you think there are only Elders in New York City?" Kaiden asked, deliberately mocking. "That because there is some upheaval there, we are safe from them now and forever?" He shook his head and turned to face the others.

"The atmospheric engines still pump smog into the atmosphere," he reminded them, raising his voice to be heard. "There are places outside the cities where it is thin now, but those are growing smaller and smaller, fewer and farther between. In two generations, or three, will anyone anywhere be able to see the stars?"

"Say it is so." Maura shrugged, all rippling muscle under her layers of clothing. "Even then, you are not the War Chief we need." She pitched her voice louder for the rest of them. "Will you follow a creature tainted by the Lych-virus? One whose loyalties so clearly lie with that doomed young Archon in Brooklyn? Will you bow and scrape before a blood-drinker who's no better than a *leech*?"

Kaiden's tight control snapped. He had listened to them insult him again and again, with subtle and not-so-subtle digs at his lineage, his nature, his allies. He had held himself in check as they squabbled amongst themselves like undisciplined children. He had even stood by and let them call Tay foolish and unprepared and destined to fail, but he'd had *enough*. Fury roared through him, and the transformation followed on its heels.

"Look at him, brothers and sisters!" Maura shouted, taunting Kaiden even as he felt his muscles and bones shift, adrenaline pumping through his veins. "He cannot even control his rage! Do you see the vampire blood-frenzy? He is a true Abomination!"

Kaiden's snout elongated. Claws tore from his fingertips. The crowd began to fall back. They had heard from New York City the tales of the frenzy that hybrids fell into when they were roused. But still the cat paced back and forth before Kaiden, seemingly unafraid.

"Look at him!" she shouted. "Look at him and tell me: Is *this* the War Chief you want, Tribes of the East Coast?"

Leathery wings erupted from Kaiden's back. He pounced, claws outstretched and teeth bared. But she wasn't there.

The Puma-Shifter had jumped lithely onto the rock behind him, her own features starting to slide into the sharper angles of a cat's, fur sprouting along the backs of her hands. Kaiden leapt upward to catch her with a roar.

"Bear witness!" she screeched, somersaulting over his head so close that his reaching claws scraped across flannel. "Is *this* the Chief you want leading you into battle?"

Had he been any other Shifter, she might have made it. But Kaiden spun, wings unfurling before he hit the ground, and snagged the edge of her boot.

Maura hit the ground awkwardly, shoulder-first, hard enough that it must have driven the wind out of her. The other Shifters scattered outward to give the fight space. But Kaiden had no intention of killing the woman.

His talons, which had hooked around her boot and pierced her ankle, were still dripping with her blood. He raised them to his monstrous lips, breathing in the sharp, animal scent of it. And then he licked it from his claws. A shiver of revulsion ran through the crowd as they all saw him for what he was.

Which was exactly what Kaiden wanted.

Shivering with the effort of containing his frenzy, Kaiden clenched his fist until Maura's blood dripped to the forest floor.

"Yes," he growled, voice rumbling in his chest. "I am a Hybrid. I am Elder and Shifter." He swept his gaze across the crowd. "And it is *both* those things that qualifies me to stand here before you today and lead you.

"I know what it means to be a Shifter. To be born to the pack, and to share blood and bone and breath with family. And I know better than anyone else here the mind of an Elder. I *know* our enemy, and I have not forgotten who that is or what they have done to our people."

For a moment, he wondered if he should tell them the truth. Tell them the *real* plan. *No. They cannot be trusted. Yet.*

"I tell you this, gathered chiefs of the Shifter families. We Shifters are on the brink of extinction."

A gasp arose from the crowd. Rumbles of anger.

"You all know it," Kaiden said over the sound of their discontent. "Before Archon Maslov, before the Battle of the Boroughs, Shifters all through New York and the surrounding states were being hunted. Shifters all over the world are *still being hunted.* Driven into the farthest corners of the wilderness. Nowhere is safe for us. The Elders have even managed to burn the skies and block the sun!"

Kaiden raised a hand to shake a fist at the sky above. "What could we do? They have the drones, the guns, the missiles, the rockets, the technology. What do we have but our claws?" His voice rose. "*That* is the future that those like Chief Tol are presenting to you. A future of fear, of scraps, hiding ourselves in the shrinking remains of the wild and praying it is someone else's family and not our own hunted down and burned out of their homes! Well, *I* will not have that!

"You may not like it. You may think that I'm weak or misguided. You may call me an Abomination. That is your choice."

The gathering had fallen silent. Eyes—human and rodent and canine and ursine and vulpine—were fixed on his face. They were listening. Even the Archivist, though he harrumphed at the lack of procedure, was intent on his words.

"If you believe I'm not the candidate best suited to be War Chief, you are free to challenge me to single combat. Or set me a task. Test my skills. I will win every time. Because what I speak is the truth. I'm the one who killed Lubok. I am Alpha of his pack and territory which, unfortunately for you, is the entire East Coast. So you can challenge me or you can follow me toward the future I see ahead if we are willing to fight for it."

Kaiden leaned in toward them, lowering his voice just enough to make them listen for it. "You have until dawn to make a decision on where you stand: with the East Coast tribes, fighting, or alone with Maura and whatever cowards she's recruited, hiding from the Elder death-squads as they come to round you all up!"

Kaiden's anger ebbed, and he shivered back down into human skin. The pulsing sharpness of his senses that the monstrous form granted him ebbed away, leaving him exhausted and feeling strangely disconnected in its absence, as it always did.

He was famished, and he knew that only one thing would appease his appetite. Stalking out of the meeting, despite the protocol that a Gathering had to continue until an agreement had been reached, he walked down a slope toward his camp. Inside his tent was a supply of blood bags, granted to him by Tay before he left.

Kaiden didn't dream exactly as the Elders did, but he still wouldn't allow the other Shifters to see him so vulnerable, caught in the grip of the blood. He stepped into the tent and tied the flaps tightly shut. The lingering flavor of blood on his tongue only made his hunger sharper, deeper. It demanded to be sated.

He had licked it from his claws deliberately, not in an act of frenzy. He had done it to prove a point to the other Shifters at the Gathering: that he was different, an Abomination, a monster.

Only through acknowledging and accepting our differences can we succeed, he reminded himself as his gaze moved to the metal case sitting beside his cot. *The others have to see me for what I am, and see the future for what it must be.*

He pulled a bag from the cooled carrying case and ripped into it. It was thick and sludgy cold, disgusting, but what could he do?

I wanted to shock them, to push them. But what if I went too far? What if they really did challenge his leadership? Kaiden tipped his head back, the taste of iron spilling into his mouth. *I do what I must. And if that means defeating every chief who stands in the way of peace between Elders and Shifters, I'll do it.*

As he sank into the dream, however, Kaiden couldn't think of anything but taste of Maura Tol's blood on his claws...

Chapter 8

"Every society has its monsters, the old fears that stalk them through the night and lurk just beyond the reach of the senses. Elders are no exception to this rule."
–excerpt from *On Black Wings Rising: The Origins of the Dark Moon Killer*, by Valentine Clark

The streets under Tabitha Maslov's feet were slick with rain, chill air settling into the canyons between the buildings. It surprised her, that sensation of cold—it was so rare since her death that she felt any kind of physical discomfort. But the night around her was indeed cold and wet and miserable. Her feet ached and she walked with her shoulders hunched.

She moved through the streets of Brooklyn, the glare of the sodium streetlights and neon shop signs reflecting off the rain-soaked cement and in puddles collecting around an overflowing drain. The night sky above was gray and heavy, a blanket of dark clouds created by the Elders' atmospheric engines pumping smog out into the atmosphere day after day after day.

With a sudden thrill of fear and excitement, Tay realized that she was dreaming. She was a human, and all of this had happened a long time ago.

Tay remembered these streets. They were the ones she had trod when she first came to the city, half a century before. Catching sight of herself in a window, she saw the dyed black hair and white face makeup, black leather jacket and ripped jeans. The unofficial uniform of the Blood Dolls; those who, like the Servitors, were humans addicted to Elder blood. Unlike the Servitors, they were not employed. They were toys, momentary distractions from the ennui of centuries.

Servitors and Blood Dolls were not entirely separate creatures; many of the Servitors had been Blood Dolls in their youth. Many more of the

Blood Dolls, though, didn't last more than a few years, their dreams of catching the eye of an Elder prince or Archon and being elevated to the exalted state of Servitor proving ephemeral in the face of brutal reality. Many Blood Dolls died of anemia, or of any one of the other more violent complications of spending too much time in the company of undead predators.

But Tabitha Maslov was, for the moment, young. She had run away from her family home to search the greatest city on earth for her future, to become someone.

She was enamored of the Elders and their dark elegance, their wealth and their status. She had never known anything else. From birth, she had lived in a society dominated by the creatures of the night. They were reality and legend in one, wrapped in charisma and confidence that held them apart from the merely mortal. Tay had seen more than a few of them in the time she'd begun hanging around the blood clubs, allowing herself to be fed on. It was a rush of pleasure and adrenaline, a psychic connection that left her aching for something deeper. Something more.

The part of Tay that knew she was dreaming could examine her state, reflected in the window, and knew that her turning was close. She still wore that ancient Sisters of Mercy t-shirt, an item she'd discarded when she was chosen to become a vampire. She moved through the part of Brooklyn where she had lived when she had been chosen by none other than Archon Jeremiah to be his personal doll, before she'd changed her name from Tabitha to Tay.

Dream-Tabitha didn't know that her whole life was about to change, and the part of Tay that knew who she was almost wanted her to stop, to turn and around and flee from the city, back to her family's farm high up in the hills.

But Tay knew that would never happen. This was all ancient history, long ago written and set in stone. Tabitha would keep on walking, and one night in her wanderings she would meet the Archon Jeremiah, and their joint fate would be sealed.

"Croark!"

Something flew past Tabitha's head, and her eyes followed the shadow to find a large black bird had alighted on one of the broken streetlights and was watching her steadily with one beady black eye. Tabitha stopped, her stomach knotting with sudden fear. There was hungry malice in the creature's intelligent gaze.

'I don't remember this happening...' she found herself thinking as the huge rook or raven swept down from its perch, diving straight toward her. It clashed its dark beak and grew larger and larger in her vision.

In a moment there were only feathers, and claws, and blood.

Tay bolted upright in the inner room of her sanctuary, thankful that she wasn't like the more traditional of her kind who still slept in coffins. She wasn't sure how she would have reacted to being trapped upon waking from that nightmare, but she knew it wouldn't have been pleasant.

She glanced around, taking in the leather chairs and velvet drapes Matthias had chosen for her, insisting that an Archon needed to have some style. There was nothing hiding in the shadows. Nothing amiss. She sighed and ran a hand through her hair, swinging her legs over the edge of the simple bed-form. It was more like a massage table than a mattress, and a tube ran from her arm to the small auto-feeder at the side.

"Why do I do this to myself?" Tay muttered as she pulled the IV, pinching the skin on the inside of her elbow together to make it heal. A dark drop of her blood squeezed from the place where her fingers met, but the wound was closed in an instant.

Tay had mixed feelings about feeding. She had been using bags from the blood banks since her turning, and generally hadn't thought twice about it. But more recently she had begun to notice a strange discomfort.

It's part of the uprising. The end of the predatory society. There was a pressure behind her eyes, her thoughts still heavy and fogged by the emotional hangover of her recent nightmare.

Tay didn't feel bad about taking blood when it was freely offered, though she was still cautious after her run-in with Lubok's fake Blood Dolls. The wholescale farming of mortals in the Districts, forcing them to give blood at the blood banks... That was something else. Those who still wished to give could do so, but they shouldn't be forced to "donate" in order to keep their overlords fat and rich.

It has to stop, Tay thought as she pulled a shirt over her head. She had already given voice to the idea, that first night in the chaos after the battle, but implementing it was a different beast entirely. One she wasn't looking forward to wrangling.

The over-day feeding had been an experiment. An attempt at replenishing herself without needing to physically drink the blood. *Looks like it probably isn't going to work.*

The idea of dreaming while asleep had been a pleasant one—a throwback to the days of her humanity. But for many of the other Elders, being restrained like a mortal to only have such experiences during torpor would be an unattractive proposition.

"I don't know what I'm going to do," she said aloud. She had hoped to be able to introduce this as a method for reducing direct contact with mortals and the need to taste blood, breaking the hold it had over vampires and mortals alike.

But even I wouldn't want to do that again! She dropped down to land lightly on her feet. *What was that last dream all about, anyway? Danger? But what from? What does it mean?*

THUMP! The thud was distant, muffled but audible. It came from above. Tay frowned. She was in the renovated attic of the mansion—the part easiest to secure from intruders—and there shouldn't have been anything above her.

More smacking sounds, like the building was being pelted by something.

"What on earth is going on up there?" Tay reached for the alarm cord, then hesitated. Her hand moved past it to the dagger she kept near her at all times. It was a thin blade, made from pressed steel and easily concealable.

A glance at the ornate day and night clock on the wall showed her it was a half-hour past sunset. It would be night outside, and so there was no fear of hurting herself should she choose to go outside.

THUD-THUD-THUMP!

The sounds above were petering off, becoming more sporadic. For a moment, Tay wondered if it might be Archon Bethania's people firing some sort of mortars at her sanctuary. But no alarms had gone off, and no Servitors or guards were knocking at her door. That meant the event was localized. Assassins?

Another handful of scattered thumps. Then nothing. The sounds stopped entirely just as a flashing red light appeared on her console.

"Archon Tabitha?" It was the Chief Servitor, Matthias, his voice echoing through her chamber from hidden speakers.

"Yes, Matthias, I'm awake. What's going on out there?" Tay was already making her way toward a discrete exit onto the roof. It was disguised as a bookcase, made visible after pulling a book that triggered the drop of a thin iron ladder.

"You, uh, you might want to see this for yourself, madam." His voice sounded confused and unsettled in a way that made her uneasy. Matthias almost always sounded sure of himself.

That's not like Matthias. At all. Nothing ruffles his feathers, she thought worriedly as she swung herself up the ladder.

At the top was an electric lock, into which she quickly tapped the date of her death day. She then watched impatiently as three large metallic bolts slid backwards out of the ceiling, revealing a trapdoor.

Another lock, and then she was pushing the swinging segment of wood back and stepping out onto the roof of the renovated hotel.

The skyline of Brooklyn was all around her: lights of houses and skyscrapers, the distant glow of Manhattan. For a moment Tay forgot to look down, struck by the beauty of the city in the night. Then she remembered her original mission and turned her gaze to the roof.

The source of the sounds was immediately apparent.

Birds—hundreds of large black birds—lay dead on the shingles.

Chapter 9

"The longer a Lych goes on in undeath, the more fabulous the powers they are rumored to have: not just fangs and claws, but incredible strength; the ability to summon bats, rats, and carrion; to change shape or turn themselves into mist; to move faster than thought. I know at least some of these abilities truly exist, though they are rare. As for the rest, I hope never to observe them."

–the Helsing Papers (BANNED)

"Do you have any explanation for this?" Tay demanded.

Her Chief Servitor, Matthias, stood a little hunched, nervously, behind her. The Archon's sanctuary wasn't the tallest building in Brooklyn by any stretch of the imagination, but it was still at least six or seven stories tall, with another six or seven below ground. Unlike Tay and the few other Elders on the roof with them, Matthias and the guards were still very much subject to mortal limitations; they wouldn't survive if they fell off the roof.

"It is, as they say, bizarre, Archon," Matthias croaked, looking longingly back at the trapdoor and the security of the enclosed floor below.

Tay walked along one of the three ridge poles of the large hotel, stopping only to lightly step over one black feathered body and then the next. "Could the atmospheric engines have done this?" she asked, leaning over to examine one of the birds. "The smog...?"

"I suppose so, Archon," Matthias said, following her only a step out onto the ridge. "It's true that the city hasn't had bird life since shortly after they were installed, generations ago. But you saw fit to turn off the ones in Brooklyn. Perhaps they returned, only to..."

"Hmm. What life scientists do we have?"

Matthias frowned, confused. "*Life* scientists, Archon?"

"Yes. You know. Biologists. Conservationists. Bloody veterinarians, if that's all you can get! I know there are a few in the city to tend to some of the Elders' pets." Tay spun back toward Matthias and the trapdoor. "Just find me someone who can explain why these birds all decided to commit suicide on my roof!" *And someone who can explain why I dreamed about them first...*

"Forgive me for saying, Archon, but the Elders aren't exactly *famed* for their study of living things except as a means of increasing production. I believe Jeremiah had a few research scientists dedicated to the study of prey animals, in all their forms."

"Humans?" Tay gritted her teeth.

"Yes, of course," Matthias said, without a flicker of acknowledgement that he, himself, was at least *near* to humanity.

"Don't call them that, Matthias," Tay sighed. "They're my subjects here in Brooklyn, not my prey."

Matthias went pale, and Tay rather thought it wasn't just due to the height they were at. "Is that a proclamation, Archon? I'm not quite sure how to phrase that..."

"No. It's not a proclamation. Or an edict." Tay shook her head, completely comfortable balancing on the ridgeline of the roof, hundreds of feet above the city streets. "I just want *you* to stop using that term."

"Oh," he said, surprised enough to show it. "I see. Yes, of course, Archon." He bowed his head in agreement.

"So, no zoologists on staff, then?" Tay resisted the urge to rub her temples. *This is the problem with Elder society: it's so one-directional! What would happen if the Elders needed to counter a plague in the human population? Even those who only want to farm them should at least show as much care as a farmer would show his livestock.*

While the Chief Servitor was prevaricating, Anya stepped out of the trapdoor with another woman at her side. "I think I know what this might be, Archon," she said, bowing. "Or rather, I know someone who does."

She gestured to the tall, thin woman at her side. "Archon Maslov, may I introduce Elder Phibe."

"A pleasure, Elder Phibe." Tay inclined her head toward the other woman, a mark of respect Jeremiah had never offered anyone. She recognized her, vaguely, as someone who had been a low-ranking Elder under Jeremiah. "Please, speak."

The woman's dark eyes bored into Tay's and Tay remembered where she had seen her before, the tall woman with the tight rows of black braids. She was older than Tay, both chronologically and as a vampire. Older, even, than Jeremiah. Rumor said she had once been a slave, working in the cotton fields of the South before she was turned and brought to New York City at the turn of the nineteenth century. They were credentials that made her easily one of the oldest vampires in the District. And yet Jeremiah had never treated her with anything other than disdain. Tay was going to have to change that.

"Black birds fall, one by one," Phibe intoned. "In blood he reveled, with blood he comes."

It seemed to be a recitation, or a poem. Tay frowned. "I-I beg your pardon, Phibe?"

Phibe's age meant she no doubt had a great deal of influence among some of the younger generations, but her manners were antiquated.

"The Dark Moon Killer, Archon. It's a legend they had down South." There was a heavy twang of Southern Creole in her voice. "The legend of a murderer who arrives when the sky is black and the moon is new." The taller woman gestured with a long, elegant hand, toward the sky.

"Are you telling me that I'm about to be attacked by a ghost?" Tay asked incredulously.

"He's no ghost," Phibe said coolly. "He's a vampire—old. Older than America itself. In the colony where I was turned, they used to say he was a punishment for Elders who had lost their way. Three signs, and then the killings begin."

"How much killing?" Tay asked reflexively, amazed that she was even listening to this.

Phibe shrugged. "Ten. Twenty. He kills as many as it takes to teach the lesson."

So I'm being haunted by some bogeyman from Elder legend? Tay swallowed a laugh. Why had Anya thought bringing this woman here was a good idea? "I'm sorry, Phibe, but that's ridiculous. If this is an act undertaken to protest my rule here in Brooklyn, then I think it must be a trick of Bethania's. Something to raise a little panic among us."

"Perhaps, Archon." Phibe bowed her head. "But there will be more signs if this is the hunter. The first is the black birds falling. The second a message, written in blood. And the third..."

Tay took a deep breath and managed to keep her voice even. "The third?" she prompted.

"The first death," Phibe said in an anxious hiss. "An innocent. If the lesson isn't learned then, he takes a new Elder every night until he deems it's sunk in."

An innocent. Tay shook off the unease the words woke in her. "As much as I appreciate your assistance in this matter, Phibe, I do not choose to base my policies on legends of monsters and ghosts from the past. Still, if you truly believe in this thing, I give you and Anya leave to search for further signs in the city. Go find out if anyone has been talking about this killer of yours recently."

"Understood, Archon," Anya said. "Thank you for your time." She and Phibe bowed and bounded off the roof into the night.

"Matthias?" Tay turned to her Chief Servitor. "Just what do you make of all that? Have you ever heard of this Dark Moon Killer?"

"May I remind you, Archon, that I've not been blessed enough to have access to the Elder Library," Matthias said. "I am but a lowly Servitor. Were I to be granted full blood rights, however..."

"Then you would not be my Chief Servitor, and we would not be having this discussion," Tay said, exasperated. She knew just what the man wanted, but she had made a promise to herself already that she would not make any more Elders. "Just tell me what you *think*. Is this some ancient monster from Elder lore? Or just a trick from my enemies?"

Matthias shivered in the cold. "I couldn't say either way, Archon. But if the Archon Bethania knows about this legend of the Dark Moon Killer, it is possible she intends to use it to sow discord in your ranks."

"What I thought as well. Keep an eye on Phibe and Anya; I find it suspicious that she was the one to bring me this legend." Tay hated herself even as the words left her lips, but she couldn't afford to be complacent. The Elders were duplicitous in business and politics, and both Anya and Phibe would likely expect some investigation into them. Still, Tay had wanted to put an end to the age of paranoia and infighting.

I want an end to all of this... Tay kicked the limp body of a dead bird. *All of this needless killing and squabbling!*

However, for the moment, she knew that she could only keep an eye on Bethania, and perhaps take a trip to the Elder Library itself, to read up on the lore of her kind. Strangely, she found herself nervous at the prospect.

What if it's all a trap? she wondered, and was answered by that mistrustful, vampire part of herself. *It's always a trap. Rule One of the Predatory Society: You keep what you kill.*

Chapter 10

"The law of the wilderness is tooth and claw. So, too, is the law of the Shifters."
–Maska Gray-Wolf, Alpha of the Beartooth Pack

A part of Kaiden's mind heard the footsteps outside the canvas before the rest of him was fully awake. He snapped into awareness, a snarl rising in his throat as the animal that never really slept roared to life inside him, growling and threatening to tear everything down.

Easy, Kaiden had to remind himself, taking slow, regular breaths through his nose. He followed the sound of softly-padding feet as they stepped around the circular tent, pausing before the opening.

Kaiden tried to relax his body. Unlike other Shifters, his Elder heritage kept him constantly on the verge of frenzy. He felt like he skated on the thin ice of his anger constantly, always just a moment away from berserker rage.

The trick, for him, was keeping *calm*.

"Do you intend to pace around my tent all night, Tol, or would you like to come in?" he growled finally, when there was no knock or sound of Maura announcing herself. He heard the hiss and intake of breath as the cat outside froze, but she should have known better. He had tasted her blood, and he had her scent.

The flap of the tent was pulled aside, and Kaiden took another deep breath as the woman crouched in the doorway. She sniffed delicately at the air, so like her animal counterpart that he half expected cupped ears to twitch and tilt on her head.

She has no weapons drawn, Kaiden saw, but that didn't mean anything for a Shifter. She could become a weapon herself at any moment.

And so he watched her with a wary eye, allowing his senses to taste the air as she moved into his territory.

She was strong. *Like Tay*, he thought. But Tay was cold and undead, the iron taint of blood always lingering on her skin. Maura Tol was vital and alive, but her scent was sharp with fear and aggression. She knew very well that she was stepping into his domain.

Good. Kaiden thought. *Let her be nervous, unsure as to what I might do.*

"So," Kaiden said after a moment. "You didn't come here to kill me, then?"

"How would you know that?" Maura spat back immediately.

"Pumas are ambush predators," Kaiden said, grinning at her. "You wouldn't be staring me down if you intended to end my life. You'd have come in a back way and cut my throat before I realized what was happening."

He sat up, stretching his arms up over his head as though he had nothing to fear from her. His eyes fell on the blood bag he had so recently drunk from. He saw Maura's gaze follow and watched her recoil in horror. Again, he was pleased. "Why are you really here, Tol? And I don't mean in my tent. I mean at this meeting. Coming all this way to tell my packs to desert me? Why?"

Maura rested on her haunches, looking at him speculatively, and nodded to herself as if confirming something. "I'd heard that about you, that you're clever underneath all that rage."

Kaiden barked a laugh. "Thank you. I guess."

"You won't win," Maura said. "I came here to stop you because you're going to fail."

Kaiden half-smiled to himself. "The number of times people have said that to me in my life and have later come to regret it is incredibly high."

Maura watched him with steady green eyes. "You say that, but you know it's true. There is no way the tribes and packs will follow you in this, and no way that your little vampire can withstand what is coming."

"What *is* coming?" Kaiden's eyes narrowed.

Maura's shoulders rippled, cat-like, in a shrug. "New York will turn on her for daring to turn off the atmospheric engines. The Rats know it. You *should* know it. But here you are, trying to enlist the help of all those Shifters out there in securing her throne. It's not going to happen." She shook her head. "Everyone out there has lost someone to the Elders, has seen families or friends rounded up and taken away. They're not going to help one of them, not for some half-baked dream."

"Is *that* why you came?" Kaiden bared his teeth at her. "To tell me that I'm a failure?"

"No." Maura's smile was as vicious as his. "I came to offer you an opportunity and, if you fail, to be here so I can pick up the pieces before anyone else does."

"So you have designs on my position, then?" Kaiden laughed. "I should have known. You came here to make yourself look strong, to act big and tough in front of Larson and the rest. You hope, what? That they'll give you the Alpha position without a fight?"

Kaiden's mirth evaporated like rain in the hot sun. "If you think you'll be handed that title freely, think again, *Cat*. You know the rule: you have to defeat your challenger in order to win the position, and I don't think you're capable of that."

"Not yet," Maura agreed, eyes narrowing. "But when you try to unify the packs and half of them stay back here, refusing your command, some of those will turn to me, the stranger who was strong enough to challenge you at the Gathering. Maybe we'll fight, then. Or maybe—and I think this one's the winner—you'll be so busy trying to shore up the failing regime of that leech queen that you'll turn your back and let me take my new tribe back into the wilds, away from the taint of the cities."

Kaiden growled. "So this is the opportunity you offer me? To give up all those who would rather wait around in the wilds until they're hunted to extinction? To split the eastern tribes into factions?" Kaiden flexed his shoulders. Inside, the beast howled for blood.

"No," the Cat-woman said. "That's not what I came here to offer you. Ultimatums aren't my style." She held his gaze. "I offer facts, and these are the facts I see in your situation, Kaiden: You are an Abomination, clinging desperately to an outdated position in an attempt to hold on to some kind of status with a people who no longer accept you. You will lead many to their deaths, and many others will split of their own will, choosing to follow me west, becoming a new, central-north tribe. We will carve out our own territory in the wilds away from the big cities, and we will defend it when the Elders come."

"But?" Kaiden prompted, hearing the unspoken word in her speech.

"But I'm willing to concede my position," she said. "*If* you are truly as strong as you claim to be."

"I thought we discussed your inability to beat me in a fight," Kaiden said. "You saw how it happened today. Next time, I won't hold back."

Maura hissed at him, scorn flashing in her eyes. "Why do I need to fight you when you're going to throw your life away down there in the city for somone else anyway? You've sold your soul to the leeches, and they'll come calling for what's due. All I have to do is wait."

She was angry, Kaiden saw suddenly. Not because he held the position of War Chief, but because he had chosen Tay. Because he was willing to cast aside the Shifter heritage she so clearly and passionately loved.

They cast me aside first! he wanted to snarl at her. *They used me and threw me away!* But he swallowed the words before they could reach his lips, unwilling to wail before her like an abandoned child.

"You've said a great deal," he said instead. "And gotten nowhere nearer to your point. Make it if you're going to, Cat."

For a moment he thought she wouldn't answer. That his anger and hers would finally drive her from the tent. But then she sighed, and said, "Do you know of the Tomb of the Hunter?"

Chapter 11

"In the days long ago, the land they called the New World was ours. And then the ships came from Europe and brought with them the Lych plague, and we were driven out of our homes and onto strange paths."

–from the writings of Aila Armel, Shifter of the Bear Clan

The *Tomb of the Hunter.* Kaiden didn't laugh, though he wanted to. "Of course," he said. "A children's tale."

His parents had told him of it, many nights before bed. A story of the first Shifters who came to America across the bridge of land from Asia, many thousands of years ago. They had been hunted by the Europeans when they arrived, forced to hide their ways and go underground to keep their culture alive. But some had fought back, stalking the strangers in the night. And among them had been one who hunted the first Elders that set foot in the New World nearly to extinction.

How he had died was unknown. Perhaps he had tangled with an enemy too great for him. Maybe the Elders had come together and hunted him down in turn. But it didn't matter. All knew that he had been a hero. Over the decades, the cult of the Hunter became synonymous with Shifter cultures. Every new Shifter was taken to the nearest shrine of the cult and initiated into the local Pack, the local Tribe.

For nearly a hundred years, they had held tight to that legend. But the Hunter cult had been eradicated by the Europeans, its Elders and secret-keepers massacred, and the location of the tomb had been lost.

"The Tomb of the Hunter is a myth," Kaiden scoffed when Maura Tol didn't answer. "A story to scare cubs in their dens. To warn them to hide their claws and their fangs and to never, ever trust a mortal."

"What if I told you my people had found the Tomb?" Tol asked. Nothing in her expression shifted.

"Then I would call you a liar," Kaiden answered immediately.

"Really?" Tol reached into her jacket and brought forth what looked to be a canine, impossibly long, yellowed with age. It hung from a leather thong, and markings Kaiden couldn't read were carved into its surface. The faded red that stained the strange letters might once have been blood.

"Have your Archivist take a look at this," the Cat-woman said. "He will know. He will be able to read the old runes."

"If it's what you say it is, some relic of a site holy to our people, why don't you proclaim your discovery?" Kaiden asked. "Use it to your advantage?"

Maura scowled. "Because if I proclaim it I will have to go in, and it's surrounded by traps. I would rather stay alive, thank you. Better power and territory in the here and now than prophecies and relics of the past that may or may not mean anything." She smiled again. "I'm sure you understand."

"Unlike you, I seek no power," Kaiden snapped. "I only—"

Her laughter cut him off. "Of course you seek power. Every predator does." She smoothed a wrinkle from her shirt, preening. "If, by some bizarre chance, you *do* manage to survive the war with the Elders, maybe I'll go to the Tomb and declare it to the world. But if you die, as you probably shall, then I'll have the Tomb there as my back-up plan. I'll be able to lead what remains of the eastern tribes there and start a whole new territory!"

Maura's smile faded. "But, as I said, I would rather not die. I come here with one opportunity for you, Kaiden. Listen to me carefully."

He made a show of giving her his attention.

"If you're the leader that you claim to be, able to unite the packs and the tribes, able even to defeat the Elders, then you can earn the blessing of the Tomb of the Hunter. Show me, and the rest of us, that you can do it. Go to the Tomb, bring back proof, and then we will *all* follow you. But only then. Only *if* you're as strong as you claim."

This is a trap, Kaiden thought. *She means to lure me away from the Gathering so that she can divide opinion against me in my absence.*

But Kaiden could see that she was making a terrible kind of sense as well. If the artifact *was* from the lost Tomb of the Hunter, then it would be proof to the whole Shifter society that he, Kaiden, was strong enough to lead them all. Without it they would remain fractious, divided, unwilling to give him all their strength.

It could be just the thing I need to pull them together.

Kaiden looked hard at the Cat, still crouched before him. "I still don't know what to make of you, Maura Tol," he said. "But I'll take you up on your offer."

"Good." She smiled, all white teeth. "You've got four days, and then I'll make a motion at the Gathering that we disband the Eastern War Tribe. Return by then, *with* proof, and you'll have your army." She rose and turned to go.

"And if I don't?" Kaiden growled.

"Then I'm sure you will be dead, or near enough, and you'll hardly be concerned about leading the tribes."

"Where is the Tomb?" Kaiden asked.

Maura dropped a rolled-up paper in his lap and gave him a flirtatious wink. "A pleasure to meet you, Sir Wolf. Or should it be Sir Bat?"

With a twist and a turn the were-puma was gone from his tent, leaving nothing behind but her scent and the relic canine.

Chapter 12

"The legend of the Dark Moon Killer is a warning, meant to frighten those who would presume to bring change to the society of the undying. It tells us that we are not actors, but the acted-upon. We are bound by tradition set in place long ago, and to step outside those boundaries is to risk annihilation."

–from the journals of Nathaniel Lane (BANNED)

The figure detached itself from the shadows where it had been waiting, slipping down onto the darkened, rain-slick street, and crossing to the gate on the other side.

The Archives of the Elders in New York had a few locations, and all of them were a well-kept secret of the Archons and their closest confidants. Tay had been given the location when she became an Archon and hadn't told them she already knew it. She had, after all, been once been Jeremiah's personal pet.

Every Elder-held city on the globe had an Archive, maintained by nominally neutral Elders and open to all those of appropriate rank who wished to learn of their history. The knowledge had been deemed far too important to place in the hands of any one Archon or faction, and so, though access to it was restricted, no Archon was barred from entering.

Tay wore her leather jacket, a soft black hoody beneath. In her ripped dark jeans and metal-studded biker boots, she looked like any other Blood Doll as she crossed the threshold of the oldest cemetery in New York, boots splashing in the muck.

Above her, the statues of previous great dead loomed and watched. Deceased mayors, presidents, even a few Archons...

Something croaked from the black fingers of the trees, dim in the gloom.

"What was that?" Tay murmured, memories of her dream welling up and bringing with them a sharp edge of fear. But there was no more sound, no sign of anything in the murk. It was always murky in the city, thanks to the atmospheric engines. Always murky and almost always raining, despite Tay's dismantling of the engines on her own turf.

The central mausoleum, built of white stone that had long since faded to ashy, dirt-streaked gray, reared ahead of her, its simple black iron gate ajar. Tay reached for the holster of her gun, wondering if her enemies had arrived before her.

A rustle came from inside, a patch of lighter darkness detaching itself from the deeper shadows to either side of the gate. Tay tensed.

"Weapons, Archon," hissed a voice, and there, illuminated by the dim fragments of streetlight, emerged a figure in black robes and hood. The robes were worn and obviously ancient, the pale skin of chin and cheek as papery and crinkled as an elephant's.

Tay hesitated, then reached to her side to draw her short sword and her pistol. The Librarian took her weapons without comment, sliding them into the darkness under his robe, and then pulled the iron gate open as he walked into the darkness beyond.

Here goes. Tay followed, even her virus-enhanced eyes adjusting only partially as they plunged into the darkness. She could smell the Librarian in front of her: an ancient being, possibly as old as the city itself, charged with maintaining the records and nothing else, supplied with blood to keep it alive. The Librarians had no need for politics, no interest in mortals or the threat of Shifters.

She could smell, too, the dusty air, heavy with hints of mildew and the rot and mold of the cemetery ground. As they went deeper, the off-vanilla scent of slowly decaying paper grew stronger, and with it came the tang of oil and leather. Tay had never been inside, had only waited out in the cemetery as Jeremiah descended into the depths for some bit of knowledge or other.

The walls around them were close, and soon the air became bone-dry and a touch cold as the stairs descended deeper and deeper into the earth below the city. Tay gave up counting past 500, and instead relied on her ears and nose to give her direction. The Librarian, it seemed, did not need or believe in light down here, at least in the entryway. Tay wondered how long he had been trapped in the library, walking the endless stone passages, and whether he knew every step and stone by heart.

Finally the ground levelled out, and under the scents of paper and ink was a fresh, mineral smell of rock and water. The Librarian slowed, shuffled to one side, and with a hiss light blossomed from a small lamp held firm in its metal holder.

"Here," the Librarian said, pointing to the chamber that opened in front of them—round, made of dressed stone, and lined with book-shelves. Tay leaned back, her eyes following the columns that supported the roof up and up and up.

How many stories is that? How far down did we come? All sense of direction and depth were lost to her as the Librarian led her to the sin-gular lectern in the center of the room, where a book bigger than any book she had ever seen sat.

Tay watched the Librarian push open the leather cover and held up the lantern for him to see by. She wondered, a little giddily, if he had ever heard of a computer.

"Subject," the Librarian's dry voice intoned.

"Superstitions," Tay said.

There was something like a quiver from the Librarian, a shake of the shoulders. "This is a record of *law* and *history*, Archon," the creature hissed.

"Legends, then. Or History. The Legend of the Dark Moon Killer," Tay sighed.

"Elders *are* legendary. They have no need for myths," the Librarian chided, but started to flick through the heavy vellum pages nevertheless—claws on the ends of long, bony fingers scraping down along the entries. Tay peered over the Librarian's shoulder, watching the subjects and shelf numbers go by.

"Shelf 462," the Librarian said, pointing up over their heads to where a library ladder on runners extended into the vaults above.

"Thank you," Tay murmured.

She walked around the curve of the room and seized the metal ladder, her boots clanging as she climbed up, up, and up, until she found shelf 462. The lectern and the Librarian were small below her, the lamp just a dim glow, but her eyes still took in enough light to see by as she scanned the titles of the leather-bound books that stuffed the thin shelf in front of her.

Accounts of the Dark Moon Killer. The Legend of the Dark Moon Killer. On Black Wings Rising: The Origins of the Dark Moon Killer.

The book wasn't large, but it was awkward to manage as she perched on the ladder, flicking through pages to scan-read it. She didn't think much of her chances at checking a book *out* of the Archives.

...Long-lived as our race may be, we are not immortal, and so we too, have stories born in times forgotten—memories passed down from sire to brood and onward. And so, facts once known to many become little more than nursery tales. Such is the case of the Dark Moon Killer...

...The first tales of Elders murdered on new moon nights come to us not from the New World, but from Europe even before the Middle Ages and the Renaissance. They go back, in fact, all the way to the Classical Era, in which the history of the Elders themselves is as much legend as fact. Certainly, these killings cannot all be attributed to one individual, as some wish to make them. What was once, perhaps, a rite or tradition of our people has become a tool of superstition...

...In more modern history, indisputable record exists of Elders dying in surprising numbers on nights of the new moon. Proof, perhaps, of something more than superstition. The eldest among us claim that...

...Why has the threat of the Dark Moon Killer been forgotten, then, in this modern era? Because there has not been a need for him in recent generations. What Elder has defied the will of their Archonate and lived? What Elder has risen as powerful as Caligula, Hadrian, or Khan, powerful enough to threaten the whole fabric of Archonate society?

...These deaths, throughout history, have one thread that binds them: they coincided always with times of vast unrest within Elder society. They seem aimed to dispense justice to those most perceived at fault, to regulate the unrest, if necessary, by bloodshed. That they usually coincide with a meeting of The Archonate should not be disregarded...

...Though The Archonate itself has become a legend, a memory held only by a few, there is an argument for connection. The very silence of both killer and Archonate may be a tie in itself. Perhaps with one went the other, for it is not too far a stretch to suggest that the Dark Moon Killer was the action of The Archonate against an offending District or person.

In the predatory society every Elder must stand on their own feet, and the strong can only be challenged through strength. But that strength comes in different forms. Power is not always obvious. What if there were subtler ways by which the heads of our culture once undermined their opponents? A means by which to stop a danger that could cause the collapse of the Elder society itself? Would not The Archonate be within their rights to put an end to such a threat?

"The Archonate?" Tay hissed to herself, almost dropping the book. The Archonate was almost a myth in itself—a ruling council of Archons and Elders who were sires and progenitors of every vampire in the world. They secretly ruled Elder society (or so it was rumored) from whatever fortress they had devised for themselves. Tweaking invisible strings, manipulating their progeny over centuries or even millennia.

It was, of course, absurd. There was no proof an Elder could even live that long.

This book is suggesting that a secret cabal of vampiric elite have sent their millennia-old assassin to New York to kill me. Tay shook her head. "This has to be madness."

Still, she needed to know what the signs were. She flipped onward.

Legend tells that before a judgement was made, The Archonate would give their offending victim three warnings. The first would be the delivery of a dead carrion bird—crow, rook, or raven—signaling their fall from the dark society. The second sign would be a message in blood, laying out the victim's crimes. The third sign, and the most appalling: the death of an Elder who had committed no crime, a sacrifice to indicate what was to come.

If, after the three signs had been delivered, the criminal had not repented, The Archonate itself would conduct a cull of the rebel and their forces, not stopping until they and all who supported them were eradicated.

Chapter 13

"There are few places considered sacred in the Predatory Society, but among those is most certainly included the Archives of the Elders. Restricted to the Archons and the most ancient and respected members of vampire society, they are a repository of knowledge unmatched by any collection except
perhaps the Library of Alexandria."
–excerpt from *Blood and Iron: The History of the Archons*, by Valentine Clark

By the time Tay had returned the book and reached the bottom of the ladder, she was fuming. Her claws pricked at her palms as her hands curled into fists.

Is this what I'm to believe? Someone dumps a load of dead birds on my sanctuary and I'm supposed to just capitulate immediately?

Tay was becoming ever more convinced that this was some trick of Bethania's, designed to spook the District of Brooklyn and cause more rebellion across her territory. *She means to scare us, destabilize my forces, and then invade!* Tay reined in her anger, looking toward the lectern with its book still open to the same page. There was no Librarian in sight. The lantern sat peaceably on the floor, as though the ancient creature had simply vanished into thin air.

"Maybe he has," Tay muttered, trying to shake the uneasy feeling that had settled over her in the underground room. "All of this has to change," she muttered to herself, stalking toward the lectern. "All of these secret, hidden kingdoms and cults, all of these people manipulating others from the shadows..."

She stopped to pick up the lamp, sure that she was going to get lost in the darkness without her guide.

"What a waste of time," she growled. She smelled the fading vellum of the paper, the leather of the books, the oil in the lamp, and blood, old and tired. Her steps faltered.

What? Blood? Tay sniffed the air again, knowing that she couldn't fool her body. The vampire in her knew. It always knew. Unerringly it pulled her toward the exit, where the iron scent of blood was growing closer and stronger, and then the light of the lamp was illuminating a bundle of rags on the floor.

No. Tay realized. *Not rags. The Librarian.*

The Librarian looked hideously small in the light, his carefully mended robes splattered with blood and gray with dust. One pale arm, little bigger than a bare winter branch, was flung out onto the ground, its skin a mottling of gray and white. The scent of blood was strong and Tay gingerly reached down, tugging at a fold in the robe.

As the light came nearer she saw, illuminated, how he had died: A blade pierced the Librarian's heart.

Tay recognized the hilt of it immediately. It was her own short-sword, driven through the heart of the Librarian, stapling the creature to the floor. But that wasn't even the worst of it. The head of the Librarian—itself a shriveled, cadaverous thing—was separated from its parent body and set atop its corpse. The blade through the heart, the decapitation, both were elements of the traditional form of execution for an Elder.

But why? Tay looked down and saw, written across the Librarian's forehead in his own blood, one word. *Heretic.*

Tay felt cold, frozen in place. Who could have done such a thing? She couldn't ignore the implications of the body, the message left behind.

"A message in blood," Tay whispered, remembering the croak of a carrion bird outside. Had The Archonate's ancient assassin been there already, waiting for her to go inside? Or had it followed her from her sanctuary, waiting for a chance to deliver its message?

Heretic. Not traitor or rebel, a part of Tay thought. *They know. It knows.* Somehow, the killer knew that she wanted to do far more than just rebel against the wishes of the other Archons. Somehow, they knew she wished to turn her back on the entire predatory society.

It could still be here! Tay seized the blade from the Librarian's body, drawing it forth. "Show yourself, coward! I'm not afraid of you!" she called into the dark.

What was that she heard? Was it a scuffling, a rustle of something just out of sight? Tay crouched, bringing up her dripping blade to point forward, her eyes searching the shadows.

The truth, though, is that I am *afraid.* How had another Elder snuck past her and killed the Librarian without making a sound? How had they taken his head and thrust her short-sword through his heart and not even dropped the lamp, but set it safely on the floor?

There was a tramping of boots, the creak of the gate far, far above.

"Halt!" she shouted again, though if he had already reached the gate he was long out of her reach. She rose to her full height, chin lifted, and bared her teeth in a snarl. "Face me and pay for what you have done!"

Chapter 14

"Archons may war and one of them win, but everyone in reach of their wrath loses."
–Servitor saying

Tay stood, staring into the dark, waiting. The only response was the sound of boots on the stairs. They were running, getting closer. Tay smelled vampire blood, human blood, some seven or eight people coming her way. *More of them? Is the Dark Moon Killer a group?*

She rolled her shoulders back, sinking into a combat stance, and wished she'd had time to find her gun.

"Archon Maslov!" cried a voice she would recognize anywhere.

Not the Dark Moon Killer. But just as dangerous if I'm not careful. "Archon Bethania," Tay growled, seeing the line of Servitor guards approaching, their guns held low in front of them, all aimed at her. She could dodge a few, maybe, but some of them would hit her and they would *hurt*.

I wonder if I can get to Bethania before they kill me. Tay gripped the hilt of her blade tighter, tensing to spring.

"What—?" There was a gasp from Bethania, and the look on the woman's face made Tay pause. It was shock and horror as she took in the sight of the Librarian's decapitated body, and then slowly-dawning outrage. Her gaze lifted to Tay's face.

"How could you do this?" she hissed. "The Archives are a place of universal sanctuary!"

"And yet you bring weapons down," Tay growled.

"When the Librarian did not greet us, we feared some foul play," Bethania said. "And here it is to greet us."

Tay's lip curled. "I don't believe that. One of yours killed him, and here you come to play hero. Why else would you be here? This is all your doing!"

Bethania shook her head, her expression almost pitying. "No, Archon Maslov. I fear that the truth is finally clear to all of us. You have gone mad. Despite your current status, you are truly Feral."

"What?"

"We came here because we were informed about the situation at your sanctuary," Bethania went on, as though Tay had not spoken. "I recognized the first sign, though it has been long since I heard the story, so we came here looking for answers. I wished to know if it was true that the Archonate could have passed judgement on you. And look at what we've found: Tabitha Maslov with blood on her hands, trying to hide the evidence. Did you believe that if you destroyed the Archives you could hide the truth of what is happening? Convince your followers that you are not damned for your disrespect of our traditions? The will of the Archonate cannot be thwarted so easily, Archon Maslov!"

Bethania still believed it, then, that the Archonate reigned somewhere in secret, passing down judgement from on high. *But Bethania is old, and clings to old ways.* Or was this all staged? A play for the benefit of the two Elders who had come down with Bethania, witnesses to give her tale veracity? (One of them, Tay noted with a knot in her stomach, was Jackson.) Had Bethania sent an assassin for the librarian?

But as she considered the slender woman before her, the wide dark eyes lined with kohl and the painted lips pressed into a thin line, Tay thought maybe Bethania wasn't faking it. The more she looked, the more she was certain. The Archon of Manhattan and the Bronx was frightened.

"Have you nothing to say for yourself?" Bethania asked. "Very well, then. Drop your weapon, Archon Maslov, and submit to justice. Let the will of the Archonate be done, and their hunt ended, before worse falls upon you and yours."

Tay panted through her fangs, thinking. Bethania would do it. She meant to kill Tay right there in the Archives. *Perhaps it's better to fight now, rather than risk another war.*

"Archon Bethania!" a new voice called. Matthias. Relief washed through Tay. "I believe this is sacred ground. Universal sanctuary. By the laws of the Elders, no killing may be done here."

Tay's Chief Servitor had arrived with Phibe and Anya, and a team of Servitors from Brooklyn, and now stood *behind* Bethania's men. If they chose to fight, it would be a bloodbath. Bethania would make sure Tay didn't survive it, but the Archon of Manhattan would take heavy losses herself and likely be lucky to escape with her own life. It was a no-win situation.

Hisses came from the Elders on all sides.

"Enough!" Archon Bethania raised her hand, still clutching a pearl-handled pistol, over her head. "This will get us nowhere. As certain as I am that the death of Archon Maslov would prevent senseless tragedy, I can see that I am not going to succeed in convincing her followers of the same thing." Her eyes locked with Tay's. "It is clear to me now that your days are numbered, Archon Maslov. The Archonate itself has called down judgement upon you, and I will not stand in their way. But if you wish to prolong this, then so be it. We will respect the sanctity of this universal sanctuary, and we expect your forces to do the same. And whatever ill may come of this, on *your head* be it."

With that Bethania turned, stalking toward the stairs, the two Elders who accompanied her at her back. The Servitors fell into line behind them. Tay watched them go, feeling strangely numb, and didn't lower her sword until they had moved past her own people. She glanced one last time at the body of the Librarian, still lying where it had been left, and began the long march up into the night.

Whatever ill may come of this. Was Tay putting those who trusted her in danger? Matthias. Phibe. Anya. *Kaiden.* What would happen to them if she refused to bow to the apparent wishes of the Archonate?

"Are you hurt, Archon?" Matthias asked her as soon as they reached the surface, where she was instantly surrounded by a protective shield of Brooklyn Servitors. Together, they watched Archon Bethania and forces leave the cemetery.

"No," she assured him, still feeling strangely detached, her thoughts all a whirl. "I am not injured. How did you arrive in time?"

"Phibe, Archon," Matthias said, gesturing toward the dark-skinned Elder. "She knew the location of the Archive."

"Ah. Yes. Of course." She was certainly old enough. Tay wished she had time to think everything through. What was to happen next? The third sign?

Or was that the second sign and the third together? A message written in blood. An innocent killed.

"Phibe," Tay said, turning toward the tall woman. "What happens after the third sign?"

Phibe looked at her, expression clouded and unreadable. "The deaths, Archon," she said. "The deaths begin."

Chapter 15

"In our lost history, in the Tomb of the Hunter, lies a piece of the Shifter spirit we
have not since recovered."

–from the writings of Aila Armel, Shifter of the Bear Clan

"It is real," the Archivist of the Eastern Tribe said.

In his human form Gerry was a large man, his graying hair tied back into a tail at the nape of his neck. A beard fit for Moses himself spilled down his chest. In this form he was only marginally smaller than he was as a bear, and just as reticent to speak.

At least, Kaiden thought, the old Archivist didn't seem any less willing to talk to him than anyone else. In fact, the old man seemed not to judge Kaiden for his heritage at all.

They sat together in the Archivist's yurt, where the big man was currently prodding the coals in a small wood burner to life. Furs hung on the walls, muffling sound and holding in warmth. It was, Kaiden thought, a very fitting place for an old bear.

An old bear who seems surprisingly relaxed about the fact that I have apparently just handed him a relic tied to one of our most sacred sites. But then, the Archivist seemed to regard most things with the same steady air.

The coals flared up, flames licking along the edges of the burner and then settling. Their warm, flickering light was likely just enough to see by if you were not a hybrid. The Archivist pointed to the long vertical lines scored in the tooth, off of which sprang horizontal and diagonal scratch marks.

"Here, here, and here," the Archivist said, pointing to a set of intersecting lines. "These look familiar to you?"

Kaiden had to admit, with a shake of his head, that they didn't. "Sky Ridge," Gerry said, pausing to jot down his findings in a notebook. "What Shifters used to call the Blue Ridge Mountains. If the Tomb of the Hunter was from around the time of the European conquest, this makes sense. The settlers took the East Coast quickly, but crossing into the west was a slower process. Any Shifters out here in the East would have made a stand in the Blue Ridge range."

"That doesn't narrow it down much," Kaiden pointed out. "We're looking at a mountain range that runs from Pennsylvania to Georgia."

"It does," Gerry agreed. "But see here, Chief, this tooth, it's a map." He pulled an atlas from a box beside his chair and opened it to a page depicting Virginia. "What you're looking for lies east of the Shenandoah, between the place where these three waterways come together and this river here."

There was a glimmer of a smile. "The Shifters back then used the landscape as their map, and that's what this tooth is. It uses the old names for places, and the old markings. It's either genuine, or as good a fake as I've seen."

"The Cat-woman, Tol, has challenged me to retrieve a relic from the Tomb of the Hunter," Kaiden said. "To prove that I'm capable of leading the Eastern Tribe."

Gerry made an affirmative sound, but said nothing.

"But I have doubts. It could be a trap. She could use my absence to sow seeds of dissent, claim I've deserted my people."

The were-bear nodded. "She could," he agreed, tone neutral.

"Gerry, I don't know what action to take," Kaiden admitted.

"No one does, Chief Kaiden," the Archivist said with a wry smile. "It's true that, were you to bring back a token from the lost Tomb, one of the ancestral places of the Eastern Shifters, many would be drawn to your cause. But it's also true that unforeseen things may happen while you're gone. The Elders might attack. New York might fall. Maura Tol might move against you." Gerry shrugged. "You've a great weight of

history in the making on your shoulders, Chief Kaiden, and I don't en-
vy you your destiny."

Thanks. A great help. Kaiden sighed, looking down at the tooth in
his hand. *Is this what it will take to unify the tribes? To save the city? A
relic of some half-forgotten legend?*

"I'll do what must be done, for the future of us all," Kaiden said.

The Archivist's pen scratched across paper, recording. "Very good,
Chief Kaiden," he said.

Kaiden rose and left the yurt.

Chapter 16

"Trust your instincts. The wild within knows the wild without."
–Shifter proverb

There was a sting of coming winter in the air when Kaiden strapped his pack to his back, holding a stout walking staff in one hand. He wore the heavy trekking clothes of an experienced trapper and traveled light, carrying only a map and compass, an emergency water ration, an extra set of clothes, and a sleeping roll. He knew that he could hunt for food along the way, and he wanted to get this done as quickly as possible.

Calculating again in his head, Kaiden totaled up the kilometers between him and his goal. A day and a half of traveling, maybe, if he kept to a good pace and didn't wear himself out. Faster if he flew, but a transformation into his beast form would risk the omnipresent hunger and rage that always accompanied it.

There are still some mortals living out there in the woods, seeking to flee the rule of the Elders. I wouldn't want to cause them any harm...

He had spent a great deal of his life in and around the city. However, Kaiden felt at home as his feet hit the trail that wound southwest through the forest. Behind him the camp of the Great Eastern Gathering started to recede, the smell of roasting meat and wood fires lingering in his nose.

In the space of an hour, Kaiden climbed the ridge opposite the site of the Gathering and looked back down toward the camp. He saw the tall spikes of tents against the dark trunks of the fir trees, the rounded humps of yurts, and still more canvas stretched to form ad hock shelters. He could see small figures moving between the tents: Shifters in both human and animal form. Somewhere behind him the call of a predatory bird rose up from the wilds, reminding him that time was of the essence.

Standing there, Kaiden felt a strange surge of pride in the people who, for the most part, treated him with disdain. He was an experiment, a latent Shifter who had been taken as a child and infected with the Lych virus, but he still remembered his parents. Still thought fondly of his people and their traditions. They were a rugged people, struggling on the edge of survival, but there was something warm and vital about them that was welcome after so long among the pale, bloodless Elders. He lingered, looking down at the Gathering and drinking in the scent of earth and green, growing things, wondering what it might have been like had he grown up among them...

Enough of this. He shook his head, turning his back on the Great Eastern Gathering, and headed into the Allegany Mountains.

He lifted his head, drawing in the information carried to him on the air currents: scent-trails of animals moving through the undergrowth, the rustle of little creatures and startled birds. Nothing threatened, and he relaxed as he walked onward.

The sky overhead was overcast, as almost the entire globe was these days, thanks to the Elders and their atmospheric engines. Nonetheless, there was a brightness on the wild slopes that the cities had long ago eradicated. It gave him a mild headache and made the bones of his jaw ache and clench as the Lych-virus reacted to the distant, occluded sun. It was one of the advantages of being a hybrid that he could withstand the day at all, but full, direct sunlight would burn even him.

Kaiden hated what he was. He hated that his condition exiled him from Shifter life. That he could never stand in full sun again, feeling the warmth of it on his face.

Though the times I could do that were few and far between, even in the Before. He had been young when he was captured, but already the sky had been clouded and polluted by the Elders' machines. The moments in which a patch of sunlight wrestled free of the clouds were rare, and he and his parents had reveled in them when they came.

Kaiden smiled at the memory of basking in the warm sunlight, laughing with the delight of feeling its warmth on their skin. They had been happy, then, in those precious few hours of escape from the dark reality that loomed over them.

A twig snapped in the undergrowth. Kaiden's head jerked up. It was not the fall of a branch or the movement of some creeping thing.

He was being stalked.

Chapter 17

"That there is some connection between rage and transformation in the Shifters there is little doubt, but it is the Elders whose fury truly drives their change. The bloodlust is insatiable, a constant thrum at the edge of awareness, and it takes only the slightest spark to wake an inferno."
–from The Notes of M. Shelley, M.D., Ph.D. (BANNED, PRIVATE COLLECTION)

An arrow zipped past Kaiden's face, grazing his cheek. A snarl burst from his throat.

"Freak!" the attackers shouted. Kaiden's teeth elongated as something bowled him to the ground, snapping jaws pushing for his throat.

Two attackers, Kaiden's senses told him as he raised his arms to save his face. *One in wolf form.* Inside him, the mutated viral cells grew and ruptured. Pain spasmed through muscle and flesh. His heart pumped quicker, his muscles twitching and tensing.

Teeth raked down his arm but the sensation was dulled, distant. Kaiden forgot why he was fighting the transformation. He gave up and let it happen.

Bones snapped and popped as they reformed. Claws burst from his fingers. His face elongated, crumpling into a snout that was a cross between a bat's nose and a dog's. Fur sprouted. His shoulders split, and from his back burst leathery wings.

He heaved upward and threw the growling wolf against a tree.

The other attacker charged at him from the left, a wooden stake in both hands. Kaiden caught it without care for the sharp point. Blood oozed from his hand as he curled his claws around the shaft and snapped it. He roared into the face of the Wolf-Shifter.

His opponent, caught between wolf and man, snarled back at him. He dropped the useless stake and lashed out with clawed hands. They raked across Kaiden's belly, scoring stinging lines in the skin as Kaiden dodged back to avoid being disemboweled.

With a flap of his wings, Kaiden bounded upward. He kicked out savagely, the heel of his foot driving the attacker's jaw back and up. There was a gurgle, and the creature slumped. Its body shrank and withered back into human form.

Next! Kaiden turned to seize the wolf that had barreled in to him, only to see its gray tail disappearing into the brush. With a roar he leapt into the air, half swooping, half leaping from tree to tree after his quarry.

The Abomination's mind knew only the hunt. Rage boiled through him, hot and red, and the scent of the fleeing Shifter's blood inflamed his senses.

But the creature below was fast and perfectly adapted for its environment, unlike the mutated Hybrid above it. It ran under fallen trees, switched back through creeks, and raced down overgrown ridges. The beast that had been Kaiden screamed in fury as the wolf pulled ahead, and redoubled his efforts.

At no point did the remaining human intelligence in Kaiden's brain realize that the wolf was *not* heading back to the Great Eastern Gathering.

The Abomination knocked aside branches, ripping saplings from the ground. Cries of rage and frustration echoed through the ravine they raced along. In an explosive push the creature came up over the edge of the rise and saw, on the other side, a clearing and a log cabin.

There was no sign of the wolf that had attacked him. But there was a humanoid figure standing before the cabin, raising a gun. Kaiden barreled down toward it, white-hot rage consuming all thought.

BOOM! The shotgun blast peppered his wing and he banked and rolled, coming up on his feet as he hit the ground.

Another blast echoed off the mountains. Pain exploded in his shoulder. With a shriek, the Abomination threw himself at the shot-gun-wielding attacker. He saw, in a flicker-flash instant, the horror on the man's face as he reached for his knife, but then the monster was on top of him. Clawed hands seized the human's head, wrenching it back with an audible crack so he could sink his fangs into the man's exposed neck.

The taste of blood exploded across his tongue.

Running through the woods, laughing as he chased the form of his father, always ahead of him.

His mother's voice, declaring that the sun had come out, telling him to leave his coat and come quickly. Quickly…

Pain lanced through his head and Kaiden reared back, dropping the body of the hunter. His paws came up to guard his aching snout, but the pain was quickly fading. His body, reinvigorated by the blood he had consumed, was knitting itself together.

His fury faded. Consciousness returned. He saw, standing across from him, a human holding a crowbar. She was small and reeked of fear.

A teenage girl. The ravening beast still too awake inside him saw only a bag of blood. Kaiden tensed and prepared to pounce.

Her hair was blonde. *Golden,* the fading blood-memories of the father whispered, swirling through the dream that tried to pull Kaiden under. *Golden as the sun.*

Kaiden remembered the sun. Remembered the warmth of it against his face, the happiness that had welled up in his chest.

No.

The beast quieted. Kaiden staggered back, wings shrinking, claws receding. The girl had dropped the crowbar at her feet and was staring at him, frozen and trembling, her blue eyes shining with tears. He shuddered with the effort of forcing the change.

"Run," he growled at the human girl. "Go. Now."

She spun and took off into the woods.

It was a trap, Kaiden realized, slumping down to sit on the ground. He stared at his blood-covered hands. *They led me here on purpose, trying to prove that I'm a monster.*

Kaiden's gaze lifted to what was left of the human, sprawled in the dirt. *I* am *a monster.*

He closed his eyes and took a shaky breath, pushing away the anger that rose anew at his realization. Anger at the Shifters. Anger at himself. Tears burned at the backs of his eyes.

The wolf he had been chasing was long gone, its scent only a faint echo on the wind. No doubt it was circling back to the Great Eastern Gathering to bear the news that Kaiden had gone rogue. But the girl and her father had been merely human. *Defenseless.*

Who had set up the ambush? Maura Tol? Larson? Kaiden groaned. He had been a fool. He raised a hand to his shoulder to test the injury there, only to encounter the smooth, hard surface of something else instead. His eyes snapped open.

The inscribed tooth, still on its string around his neck. *The Archivist said it was real.* Kaiden had no choice but to trust him. No other option but to go forward. He'd set out on his journey with the intention of proving himself to the Shifters, and now he would be going back to a Gathering even more hostile. He couldn't arrive empty-handed before a pack that had been told of his killing rampage. Now, more than ever, he needed proof of his worth as a leader.

And to get that, I'll need to be strong. Kaiden looked up at the body of the mortal he had so recently killed, and felt his stomach knot with shame and hunger.

After I've fed, he promised himself, before the dream washed over him once more. *After, I'll find my things and continue on my journey...*

Chapter 18

"The history of The Archonate, not in the abstract but as a distinct ruling entity, is shrouded in mystery. There are those who say that its members died out long ago, and that our kind is no longer capable of living to such an age as they are rumored to have achieved. Others, however, claim that it has only retreated into hiding, manipulating events within the Predatory Society from a distance through agents who may not even be aware of the true power at the top of their chain of command.

Whatever the case, it is certain that The Archonate did exist once, and that the echoes of its rule still ripple down through every aspect of our culture."

–excerpt from *Blood and Iron: The History of the Archons*, by Valentine Clark

Word of the attack at the Archons' Archive spread through the city like flame. Tay was sure it had reached beyond Brooklyn already, to Manhattan and Staten Island and Queens. How many would it turn to Bethania's side? Even in her own sanctuary the eyes of her staff followed her, accusing.

"We have to get ahead of this," Tay told the trio of Elders gathered in one of the sanctuary's private rooms. "Bethania is going to start spreading her version of events, and we'll end up with a war on three sides."

Robert pushed his glasses up his nose. "I doubt we'll be able to get Archon Winterbourne on our side now that it's come to the issue of tradition. He might have supported you despite Bethania's protests before, given your unchallenged claim to the Archonate of Brooklyn. But if he believes *The* Archonate has condemned you, he won't lift a finger in your defense."

"So our only potential ally here is Zyanya." It wasn't a question.

"Ally is a strong word, Archon," Anya said, surprisingly deferential. "But we may at least be able to convince her that she doesn't need to join the Archon Bethania in her war against us. If we're trying to deal with the Dark Moon Killer *and* three other Archons, we're done before we start. It doesn't matter what reinforcements you might be able to scrape up."

Tay sighed. As much as she didn't want to admit it, Anya was right. Even Kaiden's Shifters wouldn't be much help to them if she was going up against every other Archon in New York City. "And of course there's no one else we can go to. We have nothing to offer any allies. Even if we could convince Philadelphia or Boston to take our side, they'd have no way of sending any practical aid."

She turned to the silent fourth member of their impromptu war council. "Phibe? What are your thoughts on this?"

"You know why Jeremiah did not like me?" Phibe asked, instead of answering Tay's question. She didn't wait for a response. "For the same reason he did not like you: I did not do exactly as I was told. I thought for myself. The only answer Jeremiah wanted when he said 'jump' was 'how high?' and I did not give him that." She smiled fiercely, her teeth very white in her dark face.

"He would have thrown me out, too, if he could have. But it would not have reflected well on him to cast out one as old as I am. And then here you come, hardly more than a fledgling, Feral, and you put a stake through his heart and suddenly we have a new Archon."

"I'm not sure what that has to do with the situation," Tay admitted.

"What it has to do with the situation is that you are the kind of Elder Zyanya will have respect for. Strong. Determined. Don't plead for her aid. Give her the facts. Remind her of those things. That you took Brooklyn from Jeremiah by your own power, with the right of tradition behind you, and that you do not need to kill Librarians. You have no reason to act in such a manner. But Bethania has reason to lie about you."

"She doesn't even have to lie." Tay folded her hands in her lap, not wanting to give away her nerves by tapping on the wood of the table. "All she has to do is tell them that the Dark Moon Killer is coming for me. As far as anyone knows—even as far as *I* know—that's the truth."

Phibe met Tay's eyes and held them. "That does not matter. What matters is perception. And Zyanya is a woman who has spent much of her life bucking tradition, same as you—fighting her way to what no one would give her."

"So I write her a letter," Tay said. "I tell her that I didn't kill the Librarian. And then what?"

"And then," Phibe said, "you hope she stays out of it. If we are lucky, Archon Winterbourne will be too caught up in his own business to trouble himself coming to Bethania's aid."

"Fighting only one Archon *would* be a nice change of pace," Tay said lightly.

"Pick your battles," Robert agreed. "Preferably as few of them as possible."

"If I were allowed to pick my battles, I wouldn't be fighting any of them," Tay sighed. "I saved Bethania's life the night I killed Jeremiah, and still she can't just live and let live."

"The Archons aren't exactly known for being reasonable people," Anya said, and then quickly added, "No disrespect meant."

"None taken," Tay said in reply. "I of all people know exactly what Archons are like."

And I'm worried that I'm becoming more and more like that myself with every passing day...

"If you believe that—"

Robert was cut off by the shrilling of an alarm overhead. Screens across the control room flashed red. An unauthorized entity had just crossed their borders.

Chapter 19

"Brook no resistance. If it raises its head, break its neck. If it bares its fangs, snap them off!"
—the Litany of the Elders

"What is it?" Tay hissed. "Report?"

"Eyes on the ground say that security has been breached in at the upper east side of the borough, Archon," a Servitor said, pulling up a digital map.

"How are the barricades holding? The bridge?" She had ordered the defenses reinforced after her run-in with Bethania in the archives.

"Still intact, Archon."

"What reserves do we have?" Tay demanded next. "Do we know if it's Manhattan?"

"Archon?" Matthias interjected smoothly. "Since the battle, as you know, the District of Brooklyn has been on lockdown. The mortals are only given permits for essential movements during the day, and everyone is as safe as it is possible to be."

Safe from whom, I wonder, Tay found herself thinking. "And our forces?"

"The Archon Bethania outmatches us at least three-to-one, Servitors and Elders, but there is a river between us and only a few access points across. They would face heavy losses in an attempt to take Brooklyn by force."

"Send out the eyes in the sky," Tay said.

Screens flickered to concealed locations around the city where discreet metal hangars were installed on non-descript rooftops and anchored into galleries on the sides of buildings. There was a gleam of red light, and an almost-silent *whoosh* as long-necked drones arced into the skies and made their way to hover over the bridges, cameras whirring and weapons primed.

Long-range sensors had detected unscheduled movement to the northeast of Brooklyn, but the aerial drones found nothing there. All of the bridge defenders remained in their places on the vast metal barricades, their guns pointing down the empty lengths of the bridges.

Tay worried at her chipped nails as she looked from one screen to another, searching for movement.

"I'll blow the bridges rather than give Bethania the opportunity to walk across," she said abruptly, the anxiety that was building in her chest feeling too much like a warning to ignore. "Prepare the demolition teams."

"Archon," Matthias ventured, mild alarm in his expression. "That would cut us off completely."

"Send the message," Tay snapped. "Prepare the teams."

Matthias sighed and bowed his head. "As you wish, Archon."

Tay found her thoughts turning back to Kaiden. Where was he at that very moment? Was he thinking of her, too, she wondered. Had he succeeded in persuading his new pack to join forces with Brooklyn?

"Archon," one of the console Servitors said, breaking the silence. "We have movement on the bridges."

Views on the screens shifted, the drones she had sent out earlier playing their part. The images wavered slightly with the motion of propellers that kept the machines hovering in the sky.

Every Archon in New York City used drones, but the idea had been Jeremiah's in the beginning. He had loved technology even as he surrounded himself with the elegance of bygone days in an attempt to legitimize himself with the others. And for all their airs, the rest of the Archons had certainly been glad enough to pick up the tech. But none of them had used it as effectively as Jeremiah. None of them had built up the same arsenal.

Jeremiah had used his drones to burn huge swathes of his own District to the ground during the culls and uprisings. He had terrorized people with them. Despite that, Tay had to admit that she was grateful for the mechanical support, and she was prepared to use it in whatever way was necessary to save Brooklyn.

She wondered if, somewhere in his derangement, Jeremiah had thought the same thing.

On the screens, the cameras followed blocky shapes moving up to the opposite end of the bridge.

"What are they?" Tay asked aloud. "Cars? Vans?"

"One moment, Archon. We can get a scan..." One of the Servitors punched in a string of pre-programmed controls that made the drones' feed wash with red, followed by blue and then green. The red showed large heat build-ups around the location of the engine blocks. The blue revealed electrical charges tracing through the mechanical forms like veins and arteries. The green put it all together with a low-light filter.

"They're... security vans?" Tay murmured, watching them line up, filling the Manhattan end of the bridge.

"Bank transports. Personnel carriers." Matthias nodded, as confused as she was.

Whatever the exact composition of the vehicle fleet, the result was obvious: a moveable wall of metal lined up across the Manhattan ends of Brooklyn's bridges. Each vehicle had a metal shield protecting its front and tires, and their windows were nothing but tiny slits. The control room held its breath as they watched the heat signatures around the engine blocks fade from red to orange, and then to yellow. The engines were idling.

"If they push forward over the bridge with those, they'll work like siege towers." Tay frowned. "Are the demolition teams in place?"

"Yes, Archon."

"If they try to come forward, blow the bridge." Tay kept her eyes on the vehicles. "I don't know why Bethania would risk so many of her armored trucks."

"Maybe she didn't anticipate the possibility that we might demolish the bridges," Matthias offered. Unlike the Elders in the room, who could survive years without food, Matthias still had a decidedly human outlook on being trapped and cut off from escape.

Tay turned to look at him. "Bethania is—"

"Something is happening," Anya said. The scanners were picking up a surge of energy across the fronts of the vehicles.

"Are they magnetizing them? Electrifying?" Tay looked on in confusion, but only for a moment. The truth quickly revealed itself.

CITIZENS OF BROOKLYN! THIS IS THE ARCHON BETHANIA, PROTECTOR OF MANHATTAN, LIBERATOR OF THE BRONX!

The noise blared from speakers installed behind the security panels, deafening. There was a tiny electronic lag between the many different bridges up and down the New York waterway, but the message was exactly the same. Tay could have sworn she even heard a buzz of noise coming from beyond the walls, rather than through the recording equipment. Bethania making sure no one in Brooklyn would miss what she had to say.

"I do not like this," Phibe said.

IF YOU ARE BEING HELD AGAINST YOUR WILL, WE ARE HERE TO GIVE YOU AN ESCAPE. THE FERAL INTERLOPER POSING AS YOUR ARCHON HAS NO RIGHTFUL HOLD OVER YOU.

There was a sudden spike in the heat energy as the engines growled and the walls moved forward a few meters onto the bridge.

"Shut it down," Phibe urged.

"Wait." Tay held up her hand. "Let her have her little moment. If she's talking, she isn't attacking."

"This *is* a form of attack, Archon," Anya said.

Robert, who had been standing silently to the side, said, "With all due respect, Archon, you shouldn't allow her to undermine your authority this way."

SHE HAS CLOSED YOUR BLOOD BANKS. SHE HAS FORBIDDEN YOU TO HUNT.

Tay smiled—a small, sharp thing. "That's one mistake. Ending the involuntary donations to the blood banks is not closing them. The more she tries to twist the things we've done into things we haven't, the better chance we have of showing everyone her true nature and the agenda she's pushing against us."

"All she needs is one hook that will hold their attention," Anya said softly.

SHE HAS MADE BROOKLYN UNSAFE.

"It wasn't unsafe until you attempted to attack us," Tay muttered.

YOU HAVE HEARD THE STORIES. THE FERAL TABITHA MASLOV HAS BROKEN THE RULES OF THE ARCHONATE ITSELF! SHE KILLED A LIBRARIAN ON SACRED GROUND TO HIDE HER SINS AGAINST THE PREDATORY SOCIETY!

Tay's hands curled into fists.

"I'm ready and willing, Archon." Matthias' hand hovered over the console, ready to give the order to attack.

"Jeremiah would never have allowed Bethania to sit on his doorstep and demean him like this!" Robert said.

Tay rounded on him. "*I* am not Jeremiah!"

CITIZENS OF BROOKLYN, YOU CAN BE SAFE ONCE MORE! YOU CAN RETURN TO THE TRUE PATH. CAST ASIDE YOUR FALSE LEADER, AND NO HARM WILL BEFALL YOU.

Bethania would turn on them the minute they ceased to be useful. She had all the loyalty of a snake backed into a corner. But people fell for that smile of hers.

ANY BROOKLYN ELDER WHO ACCEPTS MY OFFER CAN COME HERE TO MANHATTAN, FREELY. I'LL PROTECT YOU. ANY SERVITOR WHO ACCEPTS MY OFFER CAN JOIN MY FORCES, AND I'LL OFFER YOU A CHANCE TO BECOME FULL ELDERS. THOSE HUMANS, WHO ARE NOT SERVITORS, WILL BE UNHARMED.

There was a moment of silence in the control room, and Tay looked toward the desks where the Servitors sat. They were wavering, considering the option that lay before them. All Servitors had chosen their path in the hopes of becoming a full Elder, and almost all of them were denied the opportunity in the end. Dead before it ever came, or kept as disposable labor force in the Archon's infrastructure.

It was one of many things Tay wanted to change, but she didn't know how. If she made all of those power-hungry mortal into Elders, giving them what they wanted, the careful balance of power in the Predatory Society would be destroyed. There would be fights and factions and rivalries everywhere, hundreds of blood-hungry new vampires descending on the mortals. The District would fall into chaos. There just wasn't enough blood to go around to keep everyone fed.

And then there are the ones like Matthias. Tay looked up to see her chief aide looking at her with an unreadable frown on his face. *He's been a Servitor for far longer than his normal lifespan, and without Jeremiah's influence he's a good man. He has no mortal friends left; he's given his life to Brooklyn. How can I refuse him?*

Tay felt remorse and self-hatred coil in on each other in her stomach. *And yet how can I make more creatures like me, to suck the life from the world?*

Bethania was right. She *was* a heretic.

The Elders in the room—Phibe, Anya, Robert—were looking at her, but it was Matthias who made the first move. He raised his eyes to Tay, and then he slammed his hand down on the key that would enter his previously inputted command to fire.

With a roar of jets the hanging drones dashed down in computer-guided trajectories, over the heads of the defenders of Brooklyn and toward the vans.

Chapter 20

"In gaining immortality, we lost a perspective we cannot ever get back: that of the man who knows that death will come for him, and that its icy hand, from the day of his birth, is never far away. There is something to be said for that pressure, and for the immediacy that it grants. There is a reason our Society so rarely changes. We do not like to admit it, but to be an Elder is to be constantly at risk of stagnation."
–from the journals of Nathaniel Lane (BANNED)

Payloads zipped down from the drones. Explosions plumed in their wake, and the loudspeakers crackled and fizzled. Lines of chemical fire roared to life under the vehicles' wheels.

"Matthias!" Tay gasped, alarmed.

"I am sorry, Archon, but you cannot afford to lose any more forces," Matthias said stiffly. Tay could sense the waves of anger that were radiating from him, the mixed emotions of the Servitors at the console. They were angry and frustrated, afraid that they would never be given the chance Bethania had offered again. That their Archon would never grant them the freedoms others had been given.

"Cameras on the bridge," Matthias said, choked-up.

The ends of the bridges were war zones, lines of burning cars blocking them off. Some of the vans were blackened-out shells, others slumped to one side or the other as their tires melted. One—the smallest, with the least protected gas tank—had exploded.

Archon Bethania had been silenced, but at what cost? She had let them get some footing on the bridge. The vans formed a second barricade, behind which Bethania's forces would be able to take cover as soon as the fires died down. And she had the excuse of Tay having made the first strike. If she wanted to go to war with Brooklyn, they had just given her a prime opening to do so.

"It has begun," Tay said quietly.

"No it hasn't, Archon. Not yet." It was Phibe who spoke. She didn't seem concerned about the movements of troops or explosives or armed forces, or even the wills of the Archons.

She's concerned only with the Dark Moon Killer, Tay thought, looking up suddenly at a camera that had registered an incursion in the northeast. Nothing had been found when that segment was searched, and there was no sign of Bethania's forces attempting to cross the East River there. No sign of Zyanya attempting to cross over from Queens.

Then what, Tay wondered, *had caused it?*

"Any sign of Bethania's forces?" she asked, an uneasy twist in her stomach.

"Not yet, Archon," one of the Servitors replied.

Tay turned to Matthias. He sat tense and upright in his seat, his jaw clenched. He must have believed he had just given up his only opportunity to become a full Elder, and still he had been the one to hit the button.

He was reliable, always there when she needed him. Always willing to do what was necessary. *I hope I'm doing the right thing.* "Matthias, I have a very important request to make of you."

"Of me?" Matthias said, turning to regard her with an unreadable look. Tay wondered if he hated her, if he saw Jeremiah in the way she withheld his transformation to full Elder from him.

"Yes, Chief Servitor Matthias." Tay took a deep breath. "I need you to command the defense of Brooklyn for me."

His eyebrows rose. Tay didn't turn to see how Anya and Robert were reacting. "*Me?*" Matthias asked.

"You are the only person in Brooklyn who has the skills. The only person I can trust."

And yet you still won't make me an Elder? Tay could almost see the thought on his face before he tamped it down, his countenance blank once more.

"I'm sorry, Archon," he stammered. "I don't understand."

"You made a good call just now, Matthias," Tay said. "I should have listened to you earlier and fired on those trucks before they left her side of the bridges. You took a risk and took action when I hadn't given an order, and you were right to do so. I trust your judgement, and I want you to organize our defense while I investigate that breach in the northeast."

"Archon," Robert aid, "if you'll excuse me, that's a terrible idea. At this time, we need the people of Brooklyn to see *you* as a leader. A strong Elder Archon in full control of the situation."

Matthias' jaw tightened, but he said nothing.

"An Elder Archon they can *fear*, you mean," Tay retorted. "That isn't what I'm here to be."

"But assigning a Servitor to—"

Tay cut him off. "They have their doubts about me," she said. "More so now, thanks to Bethania's pronouncement. I know that. But I need to go down to the streets myself on this. To see what I can discover. And I need someone to defend Brooklyn if Bethania chooses to attack before tomorrow night."

"Then hand control over to one of your council," Robert said.

"I'm only a Servitor," Matthias added. "How can I give orders to Elders?"

"You have the full authority of this chamber, Chief Matthias." Tay swept a glare over the assembled Elders. "All of you are witness to that."

"Understood, Archon," Anya said.

"Witnessed," Phibe answered.

Robert hesitated, his expression tight, and then said, "Yes, Archon."

Tay turned back to Matthias. "So witnessed," she said. "Keep my District safe for me and do what you must until I can return and take over my duties."

"Yes, Archon," Matthias murmured, bowing his head. "Thank you."

"Don't thank me yet, Chief Servitor." Tay almost laughed. "I've just handed you a whole herd of cats."

She turned to Phibe and Anya. "You two, with me."

"As you wish, Archon," Phibe said. She nodded at Matthias, almost as though to say 'well done' before following Tay and Anya toward Tay's personal suite of rooms.

"Are you sure that was a wise move, Archon?" Anya asked as the door closed behind them.

Tay paused on her way through to the bedroom, turning.

Phibe selected a heavy Glock from the rack of weapons on the wall, sighting down it before nodding that it would do. "I am wondering the same thing," she agreed. "After the Archon Bethania's offer to the Servitors of the city, their loyalty may be fractured."

Tay took a deep breath. It was an impertinent question—borderline insolent—but Phibe was much older than she was and had the right to an answer, even from an Archon.

"It has to come from him," Tay said. She met the eyes of the two women watching her. "When some of the Servitors and Elders start crossing the barricades, as I'm sure they will, having an Archon they believe to be illegitimate bark at them to get back to their stations will only inflame the situation. And choosing Anya—" she glanced at the redhead "—or Robert risks looking like a ploy to put the authority of the former Archon behind my commands. I might have chosen you to do it, Phibe. Your age gives you a high place in the hierarchy, and that may sway the Elders, but if we want the Servitors to remain it has to be Matthias, a Servitor himself, who persuades the people to back me."

"The people?" Anya questioned. "You just said Phibe would have a better chance of swaying the Elders."

"She means the mortals," Phibe said flatly.

Tay stepped forward and chose extra rounds for her pistol, then picked up a sawed-off shotgun and a handful of heavy shells. She clicked them home and clacked the shotgun closed. "Yes," she said. "At this point, with half the city coming for Brooklyn, the Elders won't be able to defend it on their own. We're going to need the Servitors, and not just them. *That* is why I stopped forced donations and the hunting of mortals. Because unless Kaiden shows up with an army, they're all we've got. And if I got every human in Brooklyn armed with a rifle or a pistol or a bloody bow and arrow, firing at our enemies, we'd outnumber our enemies three to one."

"And be the laughingstock of the entire country," Anya said.

Phibe nodded. "Mortals don't fight for predators. They're prey, and predators fight for themselves. We are the top and they are the bottom. It is the cycle of life."

"They're not a different *species*!" Tay snapped. "We were human once, too. Or have you forgotten that?"

Anya looked startled. Phibe met Tay's eyes, her gaze measured. "As you wish, Archon," she said eventually.

It shouldn't have surprised her, Tay thought as she stepped through into the bedroom to change. Phibe hadn't been human since the eighteenth century. *Does she even remember what it felt like, to be one of them?*

She yanked on a pair of heavy jeans and a leather jacket. Phibe wasn't a fool and, despite Tay's previous distaste for her, neither was Anya. Either one of them could have guessed what she wasn't saying—that she truly was a heretic, that she intended to bring the entire Predatory Society crashing down around them.

Just how long would she have, she wondered, before the rest of the Elders found out, too? *And what will they do to protect their way of life from me?*

Chapter 21

"Those creatures whose shapes we share may be only animals, but never forget they hold power of their own. Treat them always with the respect they are due."
–from the writings of Aila Armel, Shifter of the Bear Clan

It took Kaiden another day of traveling through the hills to reach his destination. Although the wilderness should have been nourishing, there was something unsettling about the abandoned farmsteads and ruined villages he passed at a distance. The silent reminders of what had once been.

His steps took him up into the high country, where he picked his way along the treeless ridges and went down again into shallow valleys dry with autumn. That first night, he slept in the hollow of a fallen tree, huddled into his jacket against the chill night air. Trying not to think about Tay, or wonder what was happening back in the city.

How long as it been since we were together? he wondered sleepily to himself, attempting to count the days and then the nights. *Two weeks? Three?* He fell into an uneven sleep, disturbed and restless, only to wake in the middle of the night, cold and stiff and ready to move on.

It was easier to travel in the dark. The Elder virus in his veins detested even the weak sun that filtered through the branches, and on the unprotected ridges it was nearly unbearable. At night, free of the sunlight that felt as though it was prying into his skull, he moved quickly, jogging down deer trails and leaping streams. The anger that constantly chased him had faded, and he hated himself for it. Hated the way that the Lych virus had changed everything he was.

He wanted to be the kind of Shifter—the kind of man, even—who preferred the sun to the night. But he couldn't deny his instincts.

The sun rose on the final day of traveling, stinging his eyes, making his head throb, and he growled in frustration. The only that soothed him was the sound of rushing water from nearby. He had found the confluence of the rivers.

Ahead a roar grew louder, becoming deafening as Kaiden padded through the clearing. He followed the smallest of the rivers eastward, to where the water poured over the edge of a cliff into a deep pool, gathering into a small lake before continuing on its way. Aspens and birch clustered around, the last of their leaves yellow in the wintry air. There was a touch of frost on the ground. Winter would soon be arriving.

We could live out here, Tay and I, Kaiden thought. It was a beautiful valley, sheltered from storms, removed from human habitation, no architecture in sight. Kaiden imagined a log cabin down below, by the lake. They would go out hunting at night, prowl the ridges. And during the day...

But then he remembered the images of burned-out farms and abandoned small towns he had passed. The clawed hands of the Elders could reach far. New York City's Archons could send drones to attack distant dissidents or truck out teams of mortals to burn out their enemies.

Nowhere is safe. Not until those who want us dead are destroyed.

He was still east of the Shenandoah River; he only had to head south toward the river the Archivist had pointed out on the map. He would arrive at the Tomb by evening, with two days to get back to the Great Eastern Gathering.

I'll be cutting it close. If he took too long to go through the Tomb itself, he might not make it back in time. And that didn't even touch the issue of what he was supposed to bring back to prove his worth.

Kaiden growled low in his throat and began his climb down the cliff.

THE FIRST SIGNS OF Shifter activity appeared in the mid-morning. Kaiden had the river at his back, following his nose through the trackless forest. He varied his pace between a jog and a swift walk, only breaking for a few minutes every couple of hours.

He was making good time, but he was still uncertain how he would *know* he had arrived at the Tomb. And then he skidded to a halt.

Scratch marks across the bark of a tree, at his eye-level. They were scored in deep, stained with old sap. *Three lines vertical, three lines horizontal.* Warning. The traditional Shifter sign for 'stop'. Kaiden wondered just how old the sign was, and whose territory he was entering. All the tribes he knew of were further west.

He trod lighter, his ears turned to every rustle or scrape of leaves. The other Shifters would smell him soon, if they didn't know where he was already.

A little over an hour later, he saw another sign: the exact same cross-hatched marks. These, though, had not been left by any recent Shifter pack. They were carved into a moss-covered boulder by the side of the narrow dear track.

Very old. Kaiden couldn't stop himself from growling in the back of his throat. It went against deep, ingrained instinct to tread on another's territory without permission. If there was a Shifter pack in the area, going any further would mean challenging them. But he couldn't stop. Not if he wanted to make it to the Tomb and back to the Gathering in time.

He kept walking.

IN EARLY AFTERNOON a long howl broke the background twitter of the bird life, scattering the creatures of the forest. It soared high through the trees, long and mournful, in front and to the right of him.

There were wolves in the area. Had been since most of the humans were cleared out and huge sections of land went back to the wilderness. But somehow Kaiden doubted that was what it was.

Another howl shattered the relative peace of the woods, this time from the left of him, on the other side of a low hill. They had him surrounded. He could either push on in direct competition, or go backward.

And then that choice, too, was taken. A third howl, throatier and rougher than the other two, sounded at his back. He was being tracked and shadowed, and he hadn't even noticed it. He released the safety on the pistol at his hip and kept on trudging forward.

The woods were dense around him, mixed coniferous and deciduous, some of the oaks so old that the boles of their trunks were wider than Kaiden could even stretch his arms.

Old woods. They had a memory and a rhythm all their own.

Growls rose around him. Kaiden slowed, feeling the hairs on the back of his neck rise. There was more than just one behind him. Three? Four? How many?

Five was the answer. And others ahead and around. They broke into the small clearing he moved through, easily a dozen or more in total, large, dark timber wolves. Kaiden's lip curled back in an answering snarl, but he could see no Shifter intelligence in their eyes.

Despite that, they were *herding* him. They padded along in pace with him, panting and growling, daring each other closer.

"Enough of this." Kaiden pulled his pistol, raised it skyward, and shouted, "I'm not scared! Call them off!"

The report of the gun echoed through the hills, sharp and ringing. The wolves didn't even flinch.

If they're being controlled by someone, whoever's doing it doesn't care if they're killed. Kaiden pointed the barrel of the pistol at the lead wolf. It stared back at him with yellow predator's eyes.

Why were they waiting? A pack the size of the one around him could easily take him down. Instinct wouldn't hold them back, so something else must have been keeping them from going for his throat. *Which means that if someone is controlling them, whoever it is doesn't want me killed outright.*

Even as he thought it, the lead wolf darted forward and nipped him just above the ankle. Kaiden yowled, rage snarling in his chest. Blood welled from the wound, and claws began to erupt from his fingers.

But the wolves were all around him. Everywhere *except* in front of him. They were hemming him in, pushing him forward, and some ancient part of him knew it wasn't the kill they wanted. It was the hunt. He roared his defiance at the lead wolf and then threw himself forward, pounding down the trail. With yips and calls, the pack fanned out into the undergrowth and gleefully gave chase.

Kaiden pushed himself to greater speed, leaping over fallen branches and dodging rocks. He could hear the snap of twigs behind him, could feel the panting heat of breath on the backs of his legs.

The wolves didn't bring him down. He could see them out of the corner of his eye, running to the right and left of him, their coats just flickering dark shadows in the undergrowth.

There was something exhilarating about it: the thud of his feet in the dirt, the branches whipping past. Was this, he wondered, a taste of what it would have been to run with a pack? If he had been a Shifter from the beginning, if he had never become a monster, would he have run with his family the way he ran with the wolves?

But these animals weren't his pack. The snap of jaws just inches from his ankles was a visceral reminder of that. They were driving him somewhere. More trees with the crosshatch warning sign flashed past him, and here and there boulders reared up from the ground like ancient way-markers.

He came to the unsettling realization that they were driving him toward the Tomb.

His muscles were growing tired, twitching with overexertion. How far had he run, driven before them? His pace began to slow, and almost immediately there was another sharp, painful nip at his heels. If he stopped they would hamstring him and rip out his throat, of that he was almost certain. But for the moment they seemed content to go on forcing him onward, even at the slower pace. The sun was sinking in the sky, the temperature dropping rapidly. His stomach ached with hunger.

They weren't treating him like prey, he realized suddenly. They were giving him the respect due to another hunter, driving him out of their territory, and unless he fought back they would do no more than that.

All of the Shifter signs were territorial markings, warnings that someone owned this place—an Alpha far stronger and fiercer than he could ever be. The pack was pushing him out of their territory and straight toward whatever waited beyond the warning signs: a place the wolves didn't dare tread. A territory they could not hold.

Because it's the territory of the Tomb...

Kaiden burst from the trees into a large clearing containing a low hill. Set at its front was a trio of granite shards, each of them as wide as a car. A pair of ancient twisted oaks sat either side, every branch of them strung with bleached-white bones.

Chapter 22

"When you become a child of the Night, you are chosen by the darkness. You are welcomed into a family that will never leave you. Only the best of you will be allowed to pass into this community. Everything behind you must be broken, everything ahead of you must be challenged."
–advice for novitiates

The next night found Tay with Anya and Phibe at an abandoned warehouse in the northern part of Brooklyn. It was one of the many safehouses the Elders had dotted throughout their Districts—places where the vampires could find sanctuary if they were caught out at dawn.

"A few more years of those," Phibe, pointing toward the silent atmospheric engines that rose above the skyline on the far side of Brooklyn, "and we wouldn't need to sleep during the day." She pulled the cord that would close the blinds. The accusation in her voice was clear.

Tay resented it immediately. Had she done the right thing, bringing Phibe on this mission? *Yes,* she answered herself almost immediately. *I couldn't leave an Elder this old and powerful alone in my control room.*

And Anya... Anya had been quiet. Thoughtful. Tay couldn't tell what was going on behind her eyes, but she was certain that something was.

The last part of the night before, as they had travelled the silent streets northward, had been run in an uneasy silence. Brooklyn had fallen into an anxious, watchful state as the sky around the bridges glowed with dying fires. Occasionally they had seen shadows scuttling across streets and the ends of junctions, but they were too far away for anyone to determine who they were. They could have been Elders out hunting, defying her orders, or Servitors seeking to flee Manhattan.

Tay glanced down at the screen of her phone as she got ready. *Matthias hasn't called.* That was probably good news.

"Phibe..." Tay hesitated. It was usually impertinent to ask another Elder their age, but she was the Archon. "How are old are you?"

Phibe raised an eyebrow. "Two-hundred-thirty-eight."

Tay nodded, trying to appear nonchalant as she gathered her shotgun shells, checked chambers, loaded holsters. "So you remember the time before the engines, then, when the sky was blue."

Phibe snorted. "I remember that even at dusk and dawn we burned in the smallest ray of stray light through a window."

"So you approve of the atmospheric engines, despite the warnings of the scientists?" It was no secret that the world was becoming colder as the sky darkened, that many plant and animal species were disappearing.

"The Elder scientists have all said that the world is becoming *more* habitable for Elders, not less..." Phibe pointed out.

"For now," Tay agreed. "But not in the long term. If the sky continues to go dark, plants will wither and the animals that depend on them for sustenance will die. Our food sources will disappear. We'll be destroying ourselves."

"That is why we have the blood banks," Phibe said. "Which you have put a stop to."

"The blood banks cannot go on feeding us forever without a continuous source of new stock," Anya said before Tay could speak, and Tay turned to look at her in surprise.

Phibe frowned. "I see what you are saying," she said after a moment.

"The plants run out. The animals run out. The humans run out. We'll be reduced to preying on each other, and eventually even that will be gone," Tay said.

Phibe nodded slowly.

She understands, Tay thought. *Maybe I can even get her on our side, when the time comes...*

"We have problems bigger than the philosophical one," Phibe said. She pointed down the street to where a group of people was moving through the shadows.

Tay stepped across to the window, hand moving to the butt of her gun. "Bethania?"

"No." Phibe shook her head. "These are Elders from Brooklyn."

The group was some fifteen-strong, at least five of them with the characteristic grace and pale skin of the Elders. Leaning closer to the glass, Tay realized she recognized the one in front.

"Frederico," Tay growled. "How did I know that he would be the first to cause trouble?"

"He is not what we came here to find," Phibe reminded her.

"I can't do nothing," Tay said. "I'm the Archon, and I told him that I would kill him if he disobeyed me again. What is he doing, raising a band like that?"

Tay felt a surge of anger and spun away from the window, stalking toward the elevator that would take her down to street level. She didn't ask whether Phibe and Anya would follow her, though she was certain that the redhead wouldn't let her confront Frederico alone. Still, she was glad when she heard the soft tread of two pairs of feet behind her. Anya knew Frederico, but Phibe was dangerous—and her presence at Tay's side was reassuring as they went down to confront the rebels.

"Don't worry, boys," Frederico's voice floated down the street to them as they exited the warehouse. "We'll get you sorted. It's going to be a very different life for all of you, I can tell you!"

The trio of Elders emerged from the shadows, keeping a street between themselves and the gang as they strolled through Brooklyn, laughing and chatting. It was a seedy part of the city, full of abandoned garages and old warehouses, the pavement cracked. Here and there cars sat sunken on their rims, windows smashed out or metal burned black.

Jeremiah never cared about the prosperity of the mortals under his charge. Tay gritted her teeth. *Maybe if he'd treated them like anything other than feeder rats, he wouldn't have needed the constant culls and the hunts for rebels.*

"As long as they're giving blood," Jeremiah had laughed once, early in their relationship, "willingly or otherwise, then it's not my problem." That had been his answer to the struggles of ruling a District. Keep the blood flowing, both into the Elders and into the streets. All resistance had been brutally crushed by Servitor death squads and aerial attacks.

And what is it I'm about to do? she asked herself. Had there been an element of truth to Frederico's accusation of hypocrisy? Hadn't she once been a rebel? A Feral, even? Hadn't she been in Frederico's place?

The band ahead had four vampires in addition to Frederico. Tay vaguely recognized them as some of the lower-ranking Elders Frederico had cultivated relationships with before Jeremiah's death. They were brutish, and at least three of them had kept their own private harems of humans. It had brought Frederico a great deal of satisfaction to lord his higher position over them.

The rest of the group, though, were mortals. She raised her head and scented the air. There was a hint of the unnatural to them, a lingering flavor of Elder blood. Servitors? New Servitors? *Maybe Blood Dolls,* Tay thought, seeing the young faces and dark clothing. They weren't blood-bound to anyone yet, but must have been lured into Frederico's service by the same promise that attracted Tay to Jeremiah so many years ago. Power, glamour, danger, eternal youth... All of the things they would never gain as Blood Dolls.

What did you promise them, Frederico? Tay almost growled, only just stopping herself from giving away her position. *A new life in Manhattan under Bethania? Or are they just your tribute to her? 'Bring your own mortal'?*

Tay waited until the group was making its raucous way through a crossroads and then nodded at Phibe and Anya to hang back. She stepped out of the shadows, making no attempt to hide herself as she walked down the center of the street toward them.

"Hey, boss!" she heard one of the Dolls say up ahead. Muttering ran through the group as she was spotted and scented by the Elders among them.

"Is that...? Holy Night, it's— it's the Archon!" More whispers. A few snarls.

"But she's alone!" Tay could hear Frederico hiss as he pushed his way back through the worried crowd to face her.

This was exactly what Tay had wanted. When faced with the actual threat of the Archon of Brooklyn, she was sure most of the humans would flee. They knew how deadly an Elder could be in close quarters, and how merciless.

But five Elders, Tay? she asked herself as she kept walking forward, ignoring the snarls. *Five against one?*

Against three. Tay took a deep breath. Phibe and Anywa would have her back.

Will they? another part of her whispered. *Are you sure?*

"Yes," she said, answering the unspoken questions hanging in the air. "I am Archon Maslov, here to uphold a promise." Tay stopped walking and stood looking at Frederico, only a short distance away. "Strange to find you here, Frederico. Going to join the front? Manning the barricades for me?"

"Something like that," Frederico growled, sniffing suspiciously at the night air, his gaze flicking upward. Tay could imagine him wondering, *How many guards did she bring? Was that the whine of an approaching drone? Is her boyfriend, the Abomination, hiding in the shadows?*

She smiled, showing her fangs. "Good. I would hate to think that you're leaving us, Frederico. Especially when you and I were getting along so famously."

"Boss?" one of the Elders hissed at him.

Frederico ignored him, a low growl rumbling in his throat.

"Why don't you lay down your weapons, Elder, and tell your crew here to get back to where they can be useful?" Tay said coolly. "Don't you know there's a war on?"

"A war we're on the wrong side of, thanks to you!" Frederico snarled. Some of the Elders with him looked shocked. Those were strong words. Archons had executed Elders for less.

The effect of his words on some of the Blood Dolls was very different, however. Frederico had them convinced of his superiority, and they didn't know enough to be as afraid as they should have been. She could see some of the Elders calculating their collective firepower. Could they take her out before the drones came? The Servitors?

"What do you think? Want to go back to the streets for an Archon who won't even look at you?" Frederico spoke to the Blood Dolls but he was still looking at Tay, his eyes locked on hers.

"Frederico," Tay growled. She thought she heard a sound behind her—maybe the click of a safety being released as Phibe took aim? And what was Anya doing? Would she be willing to take down her former friend if it came to it? *Should I give her a chance to talk him down?*

"What chances have you lot got in Brooklyn, other than becoming bait for a Shifter?" Frederico's voice was getting louder.

He's desperate. He knows he'll be punished. He was hoping he could push the others to violence, use them as shields against her wrath. Whatever he'd told them, they were nothing to him but cannon fodder.

"I won't die for you!" one of the Blood Dolls shouted, exploding from the pack and raising a handgun to fire straight at Tay.

Phibe had a hand around his wrist and one around his throat before his finger could even close around the trigger. Tay, who had already raised her own shotgun, lowered it again.

"Frederico," Anya said, stepping out of the shadows at Tay's shoulder. "Don't do this."

The Blood Dolls were looking back and forth between Tay and the other two vampires who had appeared in a blink, shocked by how fast

Tay and her companions had moved. Two of them started to back away from Frederico's gang. Phibe still held the one who had raised the gun, her hand on his throat, threatening to snap his neck.

"So you're on her side," Frederico said to Anya, his voice cold.

"I am on the right side," Anya answered.

"Sweet *night*!" an Elder behind Frederico whispered. Everyone froze at his panic, heads turning to seek the danger he must have already seen coming. Elders didn't express fear. Even the prospect of near-death was just another event that they had long anticipated. The terror in the face of the one who had spoken sent an instinctive panic through all of those listening, Tay included.

There was a rising sound like wind-blown leaves, a crackling sigh growing louder as it moved toward them.

Something was coming.

Chapter 23

"The legends of a secret cabal of vampires, ruling all of their kind from some hidden fortress, have existed for as long as mortals have been at war with the Elders. Stories of maddened Transylvanian counts, Biblical patriarchs fallen into darkness, and demon queens with the power to rule man's mind are spoken of in hushed whispers even among some of the Elders. The truth, however, has never been adequately verified. If there is a secret group, council, or individual guiding the Predatory Society, their interference must be subtle indeed!"
–the Helsing Papers (BANNED)

"What is it?" Frederico snarled at the terrified Elder. "Speak, coward!"

The Elder raised a hand and pointed. Tay couldn't see what he saw, as it was coming up the road perpendicular to the one where she stood, but she could hear it, whatever it was. She turned toward Phibe, in among the group. The other woman's grip on the Blood Doll had slackened, and her eyes, wide and dark, were fixed on whatever was coming up the road.

It wasn't Bethania, of that Tay was sure. Even the Archon of Manhattan had never inspired such terror in her own kind.

The sigh became a roar, growing louder and closer until it was a sort of static shriek—a white noise cobbled together of high-pitched twittering and tormented screams.

"Archon..." Anya whispered.

Tay was paralyzed with confusion. The roar of the oncoming thing was almost deafening, and Frederico's crew stood slack-jawed and wide-eyed, transfixed by whatever was racing toward them.

Phibe shoved the Blood Doll forward and dove toward Tay and Anya, shoving them away from the crossroads.

The noise rose to a crescendo. A mass of small dark shapes whirled into the intersection, blotting out the terrified rebels in the center of the crossroads. Tay, forced back against the brick wall of an old warehouse by Phibe's restraining arm, looked on in horror.

"What is it?" Anya whispered beside her.

The swarm spun on its axis around the group at its center. Tay could make out, at the edges of the dark swarm, the *phwips* of tiny leathery wings, the darting shapes that raced across and around each other, all trying to get closer to their quarry. And over the white noise of their flight and their twittering calls, she was sure she heard wails of despair and agony from within.

Bats. Tay realized. *A swarm of bats.* The whirling maelstrom pulsed, and then it lifted from the street and shot upward.

The Blood Dolls crumpled, nothing holding them up any longer. Their clothes were scattered rags, their eyes gone from their sockets. Intermixed with the ruined fabric were gnawed, bloody bones, barely held together by scraps of sinew. Tay's gorge rose.

How many bites would it take to have done that? *Hundreds? Thousands?*

"Freddy!" Anya gasped, throwing herself forward. Phibe caught her arm and hauled her back roughly.

All five of the vampires were bleeding, bodies struggling to heal a thousand open wounds. One and then another of them crumpled to their knees. Mouths without lips opened and closed, bared canines clacking. Frederico had only one eye left. He dropped to his hands, heaving wordlessly, and his body jerked as it tried to knit itself back together.

The roar overhead descended closely again, but this time it didn't engulf the five remaining Elders. It took the form of a whirling spear, narrowing into an impossibly thin column of writhing black as it hit the ground between its targets. And then all of the thousands of bats merged into a humanoid figure wrapped in shifting shadows.

"The Dark Moon Killer!" Phibe whispered.

It was tall, taller even than Phibe. The folds of blackness seemed to form robes, subtly red. A cloak that fell from bony shoulders to billow to the ground. A hood so deep it hid whatever was beneath it in darkness.

The creature raised its arms, two black-clad limbs with curving claws at the ends of impossibly long, white fingers. A wrist flicked out. There was a muffled thud, and the first of the Elders dropped.

In a moment it was over. Four more bodies minus their heads slumped to the pavement. Anya made a tiny muffled sound and covered her mouth with her hands. A few seconds of bloodletting, and the Dark Moon Killer had killed fifteen people. He had displayed powers that Tay had only ever heard spoken of in ancient vampire legends.

But I won't go down without a fight. Tay reached for her pistol, started to raise it. Her other hand went to the hilt of the short-sword strapped to her thigh. The Archon felt Phibe stiffen as the older woman realized what she was about to do. A hand caught her wrist.

It didn't matter. The hooded head turned, and Tay felt eyes on her like the weight of a stone on her chest. Phibe released her and stepped back. Tay took a step forward.

With a slow flick of its killing hands, the creature pulled back the hood to reveal a face more bone than flesh. It looked dead, but there was a cold, living light in pale eyes set deep into hollow sockets. There was something strangely transfixing about the man-creature, the Elder-killer. Tay wondered if she was being hypnotized by the thing as it smiled coldly, revealing rows upon rows of sharp, sharp teeth.

"Tabitha Maslov!" the Killer hissed, gesturing with one long, clawed hand in her direction. "Heretic!"

Tay didn't deny it. She *couldn't* deny it. Standing there before the bogeyman of vampire legend, she was not even sure she was capable of speech. She was dimly aware of Phibe hissing somewhere behind her, of Anya's wide-eyed horror, but she didn't have time for either.

"You have been tried and found wanting, Archon!" it hissed, making a cruel chuckling sound more like the chattering of bats than any human sound. "You will be stripped of your District. You will lose your people, your mortals, your allies. All you hold dear will fall apart before you, and only then will you understand what it means to be an Archon.

"But do not despair, Tabitha Maslov, for you are blessed. The Archonate itself is coming. They will claim your city as their new home in the New World, and you, Archon, will live to see that moment." Its smile widened, pleased and almost kind. "Such an honor has not been given to one such as you for lifetimes upon lifetimes of mankind. Rejoice and be glad! For in your final moments you will look upon their faces!"

The Archonate in Brooklyn. The Dark Moon Killer was real and he was standing before her, offering her a hideous death as though it was some kind of honor. Before another night had ended, Brooklyn would be under siege.

Maybe I should have just run away with Kaiden, Tay thought desperately. *And never been part of any of this.*

There was another high-pitched, horrible laugh, and then the Dark Moon Killer swirled into a swarm of leathery-winged bats and shot up into the night. Tay stood watching it go, her ears still ringing with the roar of its departure, and wondered what in the world she was going to do.

Chapter 24

"There have always been Hunters. Always those who fought with strong arm and steady hand for the survival of their people. Tales tell that in the dawn of the world, when men were fewer and fiercer, some of those who served this purpose grew too savage. Like the wolves they had tamed they ran wild in the woods,
and so the Shifters were born.
Others, reveling not in the clean hunt but in the bloody kill, grew twisted and dark. These, tainted by their bloodlust, became the Elders. But always, then and now, there have been Hunters—vampire, were, and mortal—who took what they could and kept what they killed."
–Shifter legend

The sun was setting. Kaiden stood in the clearing of the Tomb of the Hunter, with the sound of the wolves fading behind him. It was obvious that they had decided there was no reason to assault him any further.

What predator exists here that could scare an entire wolf pack? Kaiden looked again at the bleached-white bones on their strings. Many of them were small—the tiny, hollow bones of birds and the fragile ribcages of rabbits and squirrels—but not all of them were the bones of prey animals. He recognized the bones of a fox, and the tusks of a boar. Hanging from one of the thickest branches was the skull of a bear, broad as Kaiden's chest.

Where are you, then? Show yourself! Kaiden mentally urged, but didn't dare say it out loud. There was something about the silence of the place that felt sacred, and he had no wish to break it. *Someone is tending this place. Someone is in charge of these bones...*

The sun had set, and the Abomination's senses were sharpening minute by minute. He strained his ears, but could only hear the panting of the wolves as they snuffed the air to make sure he wouldn't return. Kaiden knew that it would be unwise to go back that way. His kinship to the wolves was distant, and as night fell the Lych-virus made it even more so. Maybe if he had been a pure Shifter, they would have accepted him. But he was a Hybrid, a creature that shouldn't ever have existed. The wolves wouldn't allow him back through their territory.

Kaiden's nose twitched. A strange scent lay over the clearing, criss-crossing the space before the Tomb. Almost human, almost Shifter.

But no Elder. That a vampire could even set foot in such a place was unimaginable.

The clearing buzzed with a silent threat of violence, and it made Kaiden's canines ache. He was twitchy, and he knew that he would have to keep a tight control over his emotions—otherwise he would erupt once more into his full shift. At the moment he needed brains, not brawn.

Kaiden still held his staff in his hands, and so he moved forward to examine the Tomb. There was a door of sorts: three stones forming a lintel and door posts tilted back into the earth of the mound, a massive shard of granite filling the space between them.

There was nothing else to be done for it. Kaiden shoved his staff into a small gap between the doorposts and the capstone and tried to lever the granite aside.

There was a creak and a crack, and a sensation of pressure thrumming along the pole before it snapped, juddering out of his hands.

"Damn it!" Kaiden swore, the muscles in his shoulders burning. He had only managed to lever the capstone out a couple of inches, just enough to reveal a sliver of darkness on the other side. Stale air wafted out.

Anger rising in him, Kaiden leapt with a growl to the top of the lintel stone and pushed with his feet against the top of the granite shard.

Every muscle in his legs and back strained with the effort. Even in the cool autumn weather, sweat dripped down his temples.

Stone ground against stone, and then with a rush and thud the granite crashed into the clearing. Abruptly, Kaiden was falling into the Tomb. He hit a dry slope and rolled, head over heels, bashing his shoulders and knees on a smooth, packed-earth floor that sloped down at an almost sixty-degree angle. Darkness swallowed him.

He thrust out his arms, scrabbling at the earth. Small rocks came loose under his hands and bounced down the slope ahead of him. Something wild in his bones—the part of him that was neither human nor Elder—railed at being caught so neatly in a trap.

A roar rising in his chest, Kaiden dug his claws into the earth. The heels of his feet slammed against the walls of the passage, scraping rock, and held. He braced himself like that in the middle of the downward slope, panting, and looked down. In the dim moonlight that came through the mouth of the tunnel far overhead, he saw that he had been right to arrest his fall.

The slope beneath him would have dropped him straight into a two-meter-square pit filled with sharpened wooden stakes.

"Someone was expecting vampires, were they?" Kaiden panted, thankful that he hadn't landed on the things. He didn't want to think about getting out of the Tomb with a spear embedded in his legs or back. He was only a body's length above them; it had been a close shave. Gently, he let himself down until he could see that the slope evened out beyond the trap into a passageway that led deeper into the Tomb. He pushed himself into a jump that easily cleared the pit, but wasn't surprised to find that his body shook with exertion in the aftermath.

Well, you didn't expect an ancient site dedicated to the Shifter resistance to be easy, did you? He laughed at himself. Despite the adrenaline still racing through his veins, or maybe because of it, he could feel a grin stretching across his face. A part of him was strangely proud that there were anti-Elder traps in this place. His ancestors hadn't given up without a fight.

The passageway ahead of him beckoned and he stepped onward, deeper into the dark.

Chapter 25

"When the body fails, the mind must fight on."
–Shifter proverb

Kaiden found that his senses sharpened as he trod further along the smooth dirt of the passage. It was as though the Shifter part of him was waking up, changing the way his eyes worked, using his enhanced senses of hearing and smell to create a picture of the tunnel around him. It wasn't perfect vision, but it was clear enough to let him navigate his way with little trouble.

The passage gradually sloped downward and earth became stone. From somewhere below a breath of fresher air wafted up, smelling of mineral salts and damp rock. There was no dust in the air. No reek of animal, as he might have expected if some predator lived deep within the mound. He ran his claws along the walls, feeling the texture change from irregular bumps to ridges and whirls that seemed to have some mind behind them. Designs had been deliberately etched into the walls and floor, but he couldn't read them.

There was a sense of the space opening out, an eddy of air, and Kaiden froze, waiting for his eyes to adjust as much as they could. The last rays of reflected cloud-light were far away up the passage, and the place he stood was cloaked in umbral gloom. Reaching out with his hands, he could feel nothing in front of him. He crouched and determined that the floor continued ahead.

Trace the wall! he thought, and took a step back to find where the narrower passage met the curve of the chamber's boundary.

Is this the Tomb itself? His heart pounded in his chest.

He felt the abrupt turn of the wall, which carried on a few inches, and then encountered something large and rough projecting like a column or an arch from the wall. He traced it with his fingertips, feeling lumps, bumps, points like...

Teeth! It was a statue of something, larger than he was, with pointed teeth, and it held in its outstretched hands a lump of wood and metal. The smell of old oil and preservatives lingered in the air around it. *A torch.*

Kaiden pulled and the torch slid out of the statue's grasp. Examining it by touch and smell he found that it was a wooden stake, bound and reinforced with metal strips, ending in a metal 'cage' where the 'wick' of wood was wrapped in an ancient, crumbling rag.

"I've got a lighter here somewhere..." Kaiden risked around in the pockets of his belt, searching for the small steel and flint strike that could be flicked to spark a flame.

The first sparks went out immediately, but the second strike took to the preserved oils encrusting the torch. Red flame bloomed to life, throwing the space ahead of him into focus.

Holding the torch high Kaiden could make out an empty, circular chamber with an open arch leading to a curving passage on the other side. The floor was paved, the walls carved from stone, and a pair of statues flanked the entrance.

"Maybe this was once a ceremonial space," Kaiden muttered to himself. The statues on either side of him seemed to confirm his suspicions. They towered over him, stylized vulpine Shifters, their snarling faces looking out into the room and the passageway opposite.

But why just the empty chamber? Kaiden crouched low and sniffed at the air. He smelled nothing but stone and earth. Taking his pack from his back, he took out his small blanket roll and threw it into the chamber. It hit the floor with a soft thud.

With a hiss of air, a pair of darts fractured against the wall opposite. *More traps.*

Kaiden wondered if he could cross the room in a leap, as he had crossed the pit trap, but even as the thought entered his mind, he knew it was impossible. He could transform, but there was no room for the wingspan of the beast.

"They're only darts." Kaiden readied himself, eyeing the rounded chamber and mentally projecting his trajectory. He would have to be fast.

With a grunt he sprang forward like a long jumper, one foot hitting the floor at the center of the room. He pushed his weight forward as he felt the paving slab click beneath him, hurling himself toward the passageway. A dart passed so close he felt the rush of air in its wake.

He hit the ground and rolled, tilting the torch so that it wouldn't go out against the stone.

A grinding noise caught his ear. Kaiden lifted his head just as something swung out of the darkness ahead of him: a stone boulder as big as his torso, mounted with metal spikes, swinging on a chain that disappeared into the shadows overhead. It swept down the center of the archway and Kaiden threw himself to one side.

He avoided the crushing weight of the stone ball but one of the spikes tore a line of fire across his chest, ruining his shirt. The boulder hit the floor and bounced, smashing into the side of the passageway near the entrance. Kaiden pressed himself low, breathing out to flatten himself against the stone just as the ball ricocheted back, swinging just over his head.

Blood. Kaiden's nose twitched. His own. There was no way to know how bad the injury was until he could move; he would just have to wait until the momentum of the ball slowed. Kaiden growled low in irritation. A few inches out of his reach, the torch flickered where he had dropped it. He was really starting to reconsider that pride he'd had for the ancestors who built the place.

The swing of the ball had stopped. Grumbling, Kaiden got back to his feet, seized the torch, and continued down the darkened tunnel. Ahead of him the circle of light moved forward as he did, revealing a tunnel that had seemingly been carved out of solid rock. The floor looked paved, large slabs of granite cut expertly into each other, but the walls were carved from the bare, yellowing rock. He lifted his head and sniffed at the air, breathing in a mineral tang.

And blood. Kaiden pressed a hand to his chest, feeling it come away sticky from the wound that he had so recently suffered. There was a dull ache there, but nothing more. Nothing broken, but he might have bruised his ribs. The graze itself was shallow enough that it wasn't a danger. He could feel his body already attempting to knit itself together, even in its fatigued and weary state.

Abruptly, the rock beneath him gave way, dropping out from under him. His claws scraped against rock with a sound like fingernails on a chalkboard. His heart pounded against his ribs. Groaning, Kaiden dug in and held on. Beneath his feet the chasm stretched into blackness, the bottom hidden in shadow. Far, far below, he could hear the gurgle of water.

So that's what I smelled, Kaiden thought, eyes lifting to the rest of the 'floor' ahead of him. It was little more than a line of thin slabs that had been laid across a gap between two narrow ledges. If he were a smaller man he might have been able to balance along one of the edges, but the thought of trusting his safety to that precarious shelf made his stomach turn.

He swung himself around to catch the edge with one hand, nails digging into the rock. The muscles in his back screamed with the strain.

BANG! The shot was incredibly loud in the confined space. It echoed from the stone and Kaiden's head rang with it. There was no shelter. Caught as he was in the open, there was almost no way for the shooter to miss.

Pain tore through Kaiden's shoulder and then his hip. The third bullet missed him, cracking into the wall an inch from his hand. Muzzle flare lit the far end of the passageway ahead of him. Kaiden tried to swing himself forward, under the scant cover of the paving stone, but his shoulder burned as he reached out, the pain leaving him gasping and shaky. His injured arm gave out, and he fell into the murk of the river below.

He hit the water hard. Pain stabbed through him from every untreated wound, and the cold shock of it took his breath away. Darkness threatened to pull him under but he fought through it, forcing his aching body toward a shore he could only barely make out as a darker line against the shifting gray of the water. He had to make it. *Just a little farther...*

His claws scraped rock and then slipped from the slick protrusion. He went under and came up sputtering and gasping for air. The current forced him onward. He strained against it.

A slope of shale under his feet. Kaiden scrabbled forward until he could scramble up the bank on hands and knees and flop on to his back.

He was cold and wet; every muscle in his body ached. He lay against the chilly, uneven rock, and the beast inside him raged. He needed to feed to heal. His bones creaked as the Abomination inside him tried to take over, to find the nearest source of blood and gorge.

Exhausted as he was Kaiden had almost nothing left in him to resist the beast, but he knew that he couldn't give in to its pull. His enemies had guns, high-caliber judging by the agony he was currently experiencing. If he gave himself over to the rage and fury—gave in to the mindless need—he would likely only succeed in getting himself killed. With an effort of great will he breathed out his anger, trying to ground himself in focusing on his surroundings.

His legs still lay in the eddy of the underground river; his upper body rested on the rock and shale of the shoreline. From the only exit tunnel, off to his left, a flickering, orange light filtered in.

How long have I been unconscious? Kaiden rolled, clawing his way up the shale until he was solidly on dry land and then collapsed once more, panting. Agony lanced from the gunshot wounds and deep into his bones. He prodded gingerly at his shoulder. The bullet there had torn through meat and muscle. The enhanced healing granted by the Hybrid virus had pushed his body to begin reknitting the torn tissue, but it would be some time before his arm was properly working again.

It was the heat of infection that truly worried him. He had pushed himself too far, too fast. His body was weakened and, lying in the cold damp with his life's blood seeping out onto the stone, he feared he had made a fatal mistake. Darkness swam before his eyes.

Is this it? Had he come so far just to die cold and alone on some distant subterranean beach? His heart clenched painfully in his chest. *Tay...*

He whispered her name, barely a breath.

If only, he thought. *If only I could see her face again, just once... just...* Darkness took him.

Chapter 26

"The Servitor must wait until they are chosen to become their full, Elder self. They must be patient, and they must show unswerving loyalty. If for even a second their allegiance is doubted, if they still appear to have any attachments to their mortal kin, kill them immediately. It is better to have a dead Servitor under your heels than to have created Elder unworthy of the name!"
—the Code of the Servitor

"How do we stop it?" Tay asked again, unable to keep the rising panic from her voice. "*How do we stop it?*"

"There is no stopping it." Phibe's tone was firm, unrelenting. The two of them were making their way back to the control and command center, Anya trailing at their heels, and Tay felt like the entire District was slipping out of her hands. In the distance, she heard alarms going up. *Looting? Or the Dark Moon Killer?*

"Chief Matthias will contact us if there is anything we can do," Phibe said, slinking ahead to check the avenue that crossed theirs for any attackers.

"What if that *thing* goes there next?" Anya asked, sniffling. "What if he can't—"

"That isn't going to happen," Tay said, worry making her voice sharp. Ever since this business with the Dark Moon Killer had begun she'd been at a loss, unsure of where to go or what to do. And that insecurity was only growing worse. She didn't just have herself to care for anymore. She had an entire District to watch over.

"Archon?" It was Phibe, looking back at her with a frown. She'd likely tried to get Tay's attention more than once. Anya had both of her arms wrapped around her stomach, her expression worried.

I'm a bad leader. She should have stuck to what she knew, only looking out for herself. Should have never believed that she had the right or the ability to be an Archon. *If I had known when I killed Jeremiah that it would lead to this, would I still have gone through with it?*

"It's not that I thought it would be easy," Tay muttered, scrubbing a hand over her face. *How could I not see that there would be repercussions like this? How could I not have anticipated that the rest of Elder society would rally against me?*

"I wanted to free the people—vampires and mortals and even Shifters—from Jeremiah's tyranny."

"And that you did, Archon, but now the people of this District need a different kind of ruler," Phibe said sternly. "And you must be that, too. Now, come along."

They had taken no more than three steps when they heard the explosion. The rumbling roar shook the city and carried into the night, and Tay nearly stumbled. *Dear night! What now?*

"It's coming from the bridges!" Anya said.

Tay's head turned and she saw a plume of red and orange rising above the skyline on the southwestern edge of the District. Together, the three of them took off running.

Their feet carried them through the darkened city streets, the fall of them inaudible under the noise of alarms and sirens wailing around them. Buildings towered over them, blocking out the view of the rest of the city. They ran past shuttered apartment buildings, derelict garages, and abandoned schools. Once again, Tay was struck by just how impoverished Brooklyn was. *If the Elders took better care of the mortals in their cities, maybe things wouldn't be as bad as they are now.*

They raced down abandoned streets and through parks, and then, up ahead, they saw people. Phibe took the lead unquestioningly, as though she were used to it.

"Quiet, now," Phibe said.

But they're my people, Tay almost objected. She caught the words back and hunkered down next to the railings at the edge of the park. Anya crouched beside her, almost close enough to touch.

There were figures breaking cover, heading toward the river. Some wore the dark clothing that Tay might associate with the Blood Dolls or the Elders. Others, though, wore white.

"Servitors?" Tay gasped. It was clear that these people were not an armed force running to the defense of the city. They were fleeing. *Fleeing toward the bridge.*

"Deserters," Anya said.

"We always knew there would be some, Archon." Phibe's voice was calm. "This is to be expected in any conflict."

And I guess that, in your long life, you have seen a fair few of them? Tay found herself reassessing Phibe. Just how many Archons had she been of service to in the last two hundred years? How many battles had she fought?

And why stay here with me?

Tay tried her phone, but all she got from the Sanctuary was static. Whatever was happening, it was big. Had Bethania given up on trying to draw out Tay's people and escalate to all-out war? And when had that become less of a worry than the killer?

"Here." Phibe pointed to an empty side alley. It ran beside an old hospital clinic and down toward the water, likely coming out a block or two from the Brooklyn Bridge. Closer to the riverside, they might be able to get a better picture of what was going on.

Another explosion rocked the night. A flare of orange and red rose ahead of them.

"The trucks!" Tay gasped. "Matthias is blowing the bridges!"

"He'd be a fool to do so," Phibe growled, and they sprinted down the alleyway, the sounds of the night and the roar of the burning all around them.

A sound of metal on metal, so small she might not have heard it if her senses hadn't been on high alert. Tay spun around in confusion just as Phibe body-checked her to the ground. Gunfire rattled over their heads, sparking off the metal bins, the pull-down ladders, and the concrete around them.

"There she is!" someone shouted behind them. "It's all her fault!"

Phibe pushed her toward one of the large metal garbage bins. Tay protested, but the ancient Elder snarled an order to move and she found herself complying before her mind had fully caught up with her body. Anya was already hunkered down behind it.

"Get her! Bethania will stop this if—" He never had a chance to finish his statement. Phibe rose, spun on her heel and, with a snap of her wrist, sent a dagger spinning back the way they had come. There was the thump of a body hitting the ground, and a gurgle that made Tay glad she hadn't seen where the knife hit.

Phibe folded herself into a doorway opposite Tay as another burst of gunfire sounded, followed by a curse from Phibe as the bullets found her hiding place.

"Phibe!" Tay leaned around the bin, took aim, and fired. There were four Servitors, all in Brooklyn uniforms, holding semi-automatic rifles. A third lay crumpled on the ground with a knife in his throat. The second, hit by her bullet, staggered back and fell to his knees. Before she could aim and fire again, the crack of a pistol announced Anya's presence and another Servitor crumpled.

"Phibe?" Tay looked over to see the other woman, a bullet hole in her shoulder leaking blood, another open just under her ribs. *She'll be able to heal herself if she can feed.*

Bullets ricocheted off the bin and Tay was forced back, into hiding again.

"There are two more!" she heard one of the remaining Servitors shout.

Tay exchanged a glance with Anya. They had to move immediately, and she gestured to the bin. Anya nodded. *Three...* Tay held up her fingers. *Two... One.*

Leaping up she grabbed the large metal bin, which was on wheels, and shoved. She had fed just the night before and hadn't been wounded recently, so she was almost as strong as she would have liked. The metal container, far too heavy for a human to shift, moved easily under her hands as her system flushed with viral strength. In the same moment, Anya came up shooting.

It was over in a moment.

The bin hit one of the Servitors, slamming him back against opposite wall and knocking his gun from his hand. The other fell with a bullet hole in his forehead.

Tay hauled the bin back from the still-stunned Servitor and wrapped a hand around his throat. She lifted him until his feet dangled above the ground, and then she squeezed.

"How dare you betray your Archon!" Tay hissed at him, fangs bared.

"Usurper," the Servitor gasped. "Traitor!"

Rage sparked deep in Tay's stomach, roaring through her with bestial intensity. The thrill of the hunt was hot in her veins, and with a ripping snarl she sank her teeth into the Servitor's throat. Blood spilled into her mouth, and with it came the dream...

Chapter 27

"The truth? The truth is that this is no new race or species. This is a virus—a virus that is alive. It wants. It hungers. And it will not stop until it has devoured the world."
–audio recording from the Hunter's library (BANNED)

The man before her was tall and seemingly young, with eyes like chips of frozen lake water, and Tay thought she was in love with him.

Unlike the other Dolls she had seen the Archon of Brooklyn with Jeremiah seemed to court her, to woo her even. He had picked her from the crowd of dancers at the Doll Club and asked her if she was ready to offer her blood. Tay had agreed enthusiastically, but Jeremiah had refrained from taking more than a mouthful. His fangs slid beneath her skin, a brief, exquisite pain, terrible and yet something she longed for. Her body thrilled with the danger of being so close to a predator. He could have killed her in a moment, and yet she had what he wanted, what he needed, and as long as that was the case she had some power over him.

Months passed. Months of on and off flirting, of delicate feeding. Tay was getting addicted not only to the lifestyle, but to the Archon himself. He invited her to stay at his side even when he was not feeding from her, to meetings with his fellow senior Elders where she was to remain silent at the back of the room, dressed always in black.

It was time. Time for her transformation to full Elder. The other Blood Dolls were insane with jealousy, Elders angered at how quickly she had risen.

'Are there no Servitors more worthy than this one' she would hear them sneer.

'He'll tire of her. He always does.'

But Tay pushed all of those words and worries aside as she accepted Jeremiah's hand. He reached out with the other and began to pull back the velvet curtain before them.

She would have to feed on an Elder. Only by ingesting Elder blood could she make certain she would rise again as one of them when Jeremiah drained her. He would feed on her, and kill her, and the virus would awaken in her body, claiming her as its own.

Tay wondered who she would have to feed on. Jeremiah himself? Another? A Feral? The curtain lifted and a big ugly bird as black as midnight flew straight at her with a shriek.

"Archon!" Anya was shaking her, pulling her out of the dream, and Tay sat up groggily.

Why had she thought about that, after all this time? She felt different somehow, sickened by the virus inside her own blood. A moan came from further down the alleyway, and Tay realized that they had to feed Phibe or the woman would die. Picking up the Servitor Anya's shot had killed, Tay dragged him to the doorway and within Phibe's reach.

Phibe leaned down over him, fangs tearing into his throat, and drank first weakly and then desperately. Tay watched as Phibe's eyes rolled back to just their whites and the dreaming took her, her clawed hands twitching.

"You'll be okay," Tay sighed. She straightened up. "Anya, stay here and watch him."

Anya nodded, tucking her pistol back into her belt.

Tay walked to the end of the alleyway to get a better view of the bridge. She hooked her phone out of her pocket and dialed the number that would get her Matthias.

"Mistress!" he answered on the third ring. "Thank the night it's—" The line was still full of white noise, and it cut him off.

"We're at the Brooklyn Bridge. What are we looking at, Chief?"

The bridge was a disaster zone. At the far end, only a few burned-out shells of vehicles remained. The rest had likely fallen into the gaping wound in the bridge, from which broken girders twisted, their ends melted. Flames still burned above.

"...attacked, Archon!" A hiss of static. "...it was, but it swept down and—"

Tay hung her head. The Dark Moon Killer had attacked the bridge itself. She heard, in fits and starts, how it had swept over the bridge in a storm of bats, eviscerating a line of her Servitors before it continued on to the other side where Bethania's forces sat. It had not, apparently, cared to differentiate between the two.

"...opened fire. She must have thought it was us, but it wasn't!" the Servitor said.

"I know. It was the Dark Moon Killer, Chief. We saw him. It's real. It's here." Guilt sat heavy on Tay's shoulders. Every one of those men and women who had died were dead because of her. Because her decisions had put them in the creature's line of fire.

At the other end of the line, the Chief Servitor swore before continuing his report. "Our side opened fire in retaliation against Bethania. If it were just the two forces, we could have held off..." More static. "There was no way that they... bridge in just a rush, not without..."

The connection was terrible, but Tay managed to get most of what Matthias was saying.

"A rebellion," he went on. "...center."

"At the control center itself? How many? Who?"

"...Elders. A few Servitor staff. Don't worry, we put them down." There was a terrible finality to the Chief's voice. "But... damage to the communications..."

"I can hear that. Just get it sorted." Tay rolled her aching shoulders. "I'm coming in. Repeat: I'm coming in."

Her head turned as a sound caught her attention. It was the hissing sigh of a rising wind, so faint and far away that Tay almost didn't recognize it for what it really was until it grew louder and became a too-familiar cacophony of wings and high-pitched twittering: the noise of a vast cloud of bats. Exhaustion swept over Tay in a wave.

I'm not prepared for this, she thought despairingly. *Can't I just have a moment?*

"There!" The word came not from her but from Phibe, who stood at her side once more, her eyes bright with the renewed vitality that came from the blood she had just ingested. Her jacket was in ruins, but most of her injuries seemed to have at least begun to seal. Anya, beside her, was thin-lipped and tense.

Tay followed Phibe's pointing hand to where the light of flames from the bridge gleamed off thousands of leathery wings, a vortex of bats swirling over the river. They separated and reformed, whirling together into a massive, spiraling morass.

There was an eruption of gunfire, and Tay and her companions watched as tracer fire shot up from Manhattan into twittering colony. The swarm convulsed, pulsating like a school of fish before suddenly diving down, *through* the attacking gunfire, to fall on Bethania's defenses.

Distant screams sounded over the rising chorus of the swarm. The rattle of machine guns was aimed not only into the cloud of bats, but across the ruined bridge toward the Brooklyn side, too.

"She believes we are the ones attacking her," Phibe said, watching grimly as dark figures leapt over burning wreckage to begin throwing ropes across the gap in the bridge. Tay's own people were near the Brooklyn edge, cowering away from the whirling swarm that had already decimated their numbers, too far away to defend against the interlopers.

"Chief?" Tay was instantly on the phone. "Matthias?"

There was a staticky crackle, and then, "Here."

"If you can read me, activate the drones. Strafe the bridge. Full deployment. Repeat: drones, strafe bridge, full deployment." She watched as the Dark Moon swarm rose from the Manhattan side of the bridge and moved toward her own defenses. If this went on for much longer there would be nothing left, and Bethania, or the killer, would be free to take the city.

The bridge was chaos. Some of Bethania's men were fleeing. Others were standing, no doubt slack-jawed, to watch the swarm descend on Tay's Servitors. Overhead, Tay heard the reassuring whine of the drone fleet. They appeared as large black shapes, flying in V-formation high over the river.

"How many are going to die?" Tay wondered out loud, shuddering.

"Only Bethania's people," Phibe growled. "It's what you have to do."

"We have no choice," Anya said, backing her up.

But Tay couldn't find it in her heart to forgive herself. The Elders and Servitors from Manhattan were only obeying orders. *Following the lead of a mad dictator.* She growled. *This war isn't what I want for this city, for any of us!*

Lines of chemical fire erupted across the bridge as the drones swept low over the street before rising again, roaring into the sky for a return strike. She had ordered a full deployment, and that was what her Chief Servitor had given her. All twenty-one of their advanced robotic drones fired their inferno weapons upon the bridge, engulfing both the rising swarm and Bethania's forces.

The glare from the flames was so bright that it hurt Tay's eyes to look directly at it, but she refused to look away. Elders and Servitors, still burning, flung themselves into the water on either side of the bridge.

There were answering explosions from the gas tanks of the un-burned vehicles parked on the bridge itself, and then a grinding of metal girders. With a lurch and a tortured groan the whole bridge sagged on one side, its surface turning to pitch still more bodies and burning equipment into the river.

The roars and the shouting went on for far too long as Tay stood there with Anya and Phibe, watching the carnage. As quiet slowly settled once more the bridge lay to one side, sections of it in the water, just a thin curve of road and metal supports rising above the surface.

"Well, Bethania won't be able to invade the city by that route anymore," Phibe said.

"I don't think *anyone* will be able to use that route again in the near future." Tay shook her head at the enormity of the destruction. They were tearing their city apart, all of them. Who was going to rebuild it? How? Would they ever even have the opportunity? And what had happened to the creature?

"Do you think we killed it?" Tay wondered, peering at the ruins. The slightest sliver of hope rose in her chest, but when she turned to look at Phibe she knew the answer.

"No," the ancient Elder said, her voice soft and grim. "No, Archon. I do not believe you did."

Chapter 28

"We have this in common: Death is sacred to us all."
−unknown

The depth of his darkness started to grey, to lighten, until he became aware of a warm orange glow. Kaiden the man was a distant consciousness swimming in a sea of pain and forgetfulness, given over to his body.

Hush, the beast part of him urged, stilling his heart, slowing his breathing. *Don't move.* To the outside world, he knew he must look dead: skin pale and eyes rolled back in his head. His heart beat only a few times per minute, and the breath that moved through blood-flecked lips was barely a whisper.

The orange glow resolved itself into a torch, a fraction of warmth coming closer. Kaiden's body could feel the warmth of the flickering torch in the same way that it could sense the light washing over it. It *hurt,* his senses too overwrought to stand anything other than unconscious forgetfulness.

"There. We found it," said a harsh male voice. It was not deep or sonorous, not the voice of some ancient guardian. It was the voice of a young man, speaking to someone beyond the circle of light cast by the torch.

A mumble answered him. The harsh voice replied, "Yeah, I reckon so. Look at that hole in its side!"

An angry cough from beyond. A curse. The beast within pricked up its ears. There was something strangely familiar about that voice, an accent, maybe, that he had heard before.

"Bring it anyway. Let's get this over and done with quick," the familiar-but-not-familiar voice said before the world spun as Kaiden's body was seized and dragged across the cavern.

The beast within him—the ever hungry, ever angry Abomination that was a combination of the hunger of the Elder and the animal ferocity of the Shifter—growled at the touch. But it refused to let Kaiden's human intelligence resurface fully from the depths.

Be still. Wounded animals hide. Wait.

Kaiden the man was still there somewhere, but all of the memories and thoughts that made him who he was were threatening to slide into the abyss opening beneath him as his body began to shut down. Only the strange genetic mutations of the virus stubbornly kept him alive.

The pain had lessened to a low, far-off ebb, a constant throbbing ache that woke once more into agony as Kaiden was hauled down a twisting tunnel of rock. This one was much older than the passageways of paved stones above; it looked as though it might date back to even before the first settlers. The flickering light of the torch threw strange shadows against the rough stone.

Close as he was to the human dragging him, Kaiden smelled the iron of his blood, heard the beat of his heart. A shiver of anticipation ran through him. The virus demanded sustenance.

Wait! the animal part of his mind said. *Hide and wait!*

There was a momentary pause in their progress, and the sharp scent of adrenaline bloomed from the man hauling his body down the tunnel. Had he caught some sign of motion from Kaiden? Or was it only his body, remembering that a predator was near even as his mind told him that predator was dead?

Kaiden held his breath and waited, like any good, stalking beast.

The smell of angry man, of both of them, was strange, too. They were mortals who had somehow managed to outfox and outfight a Hybrid. That was suspect enough. But the creature inside Kaiden sensed something else, something different about the two. It was in their blood—not a virus, but something else.

The air shifted as Kaiden was dragged into a wide, high-ceilinged space, almost perfectly circular. Through the slits of his barely open eyelids, Kaiden could make out two people. One had him. The other stood beside a heavy slab of rock in the center of the room. The walls were carved with spirals and scratches—ancient Shifter marks. The floor was cut with deep grooves, all leading *away* from the central slab of rock.

It was an altar, deep under the earth, ancient beyond reckoning.

He had come, at last, to the center of the Tomb.

Chapter 29

"The Hermetic Order of the Golden Dawn, the Priests of Thoth, the Illuminati, the Knights Templar, Skull-and-Bones… There have always been rumors of secretive occult groups at work in the world, covens of magic-users made up not of Elders or Shifters but of mortal humans. Who can say, though, if they truly exist? What role would they play in this dark world if they did?"
–the Helsing Papers (BANNED)

"Here. Put it on the slab," said the voice he almost recognized. The speaker was a man probably in his late thirties, with straight, tawny blond hair, narrow features, and a golden flush to his skin. As soon as he saw him, Kaiden knew where he had heard the accent before: Maura Tol.

The two of them had to be related in some way. Their ages were similar, their coloring and bone structure the same. It explained the familiarity. The man wore a heavy quilted jacket over a simple white t-shirt and jeans, a pair of sturdy hiking boots on his feet. Around his neck hung a talisman on a knotted piece of string. It was a long, sharp tooth, similar to the one Kaiden wore around his own neck.

Two pairs of hands lifted Kaiden and thumped him onto the slab. Pain shocked through his body with the rough treatment and, adrift on a sea of agony, Kaiden saw the other two men. One of them was smaller than the first, heavyset and wearing a trucker's cap, with a frizzy, reddish beard. The other was tall and completely bald, a shotgun strapped to his back. Both of them were dressed similarly to the first. Kaiden's consciousness flickered, rational thought threatening to desert him entirely.

Arise! Fight! Attack! The beast within him saw its moment and tried to seize it. Impulses ran along his nerves, directing wings to grow and claws to form, calling forward sharp, tearing teeth.

But nothing happened. Kaiden's body was too far gone, too broken. He had fought on the trail, been shot at by the mortal woodsman, had hiked for a day and then been chased by the wolves, and all of that had been followed up with the dangers of the Tomb. Three days of trials, followed by traps that tore and bit at his skin, exertion, and gunshots that had almost severed limb from body.

The Hybrid virus inside his body had tried to negate most of damage, had sealed the wounds and stopped the bleeding, but it could not outright heal the wounds. And in its attempt, it had spent the last of his reserves. Without blood, without food, what could he do? He had nothing left to give.

Fight! Survive! Kill! The beast within was raging silently. Kaiden felt as though he struggled through thick layers of clinging fog. Consciousness was just too far away, and his anger was just too muffled, too weak...

"In the name of the First Hunter, I offer this sacrifice," said the brother of Maura Tol, the tawny-haired man. He reached out and took up a strange implement: long and thin and delicately curved, it appeared to be a piece of calcified bone or horn, white as a shard of moon. "May its blood empower this working."

The man lifted the bone weapon in two hands, and through the haze Kaiden saw that it was covered in tiny inscriptions: scratches and crosshatches, ancient Shifter markings. A little longer than an adult's arm it appeared to be a curved spear, bound with cord at two places to form hand grips, the pointed end filed and sharpened into a wicked blade. Maura Tol's brother raised it over his head, and Kaiden knew when it fell it would plunge into his chest.

A nervous cough came from the second man on the other side of the Tomb, the angry one. Kaiden knew he was afraid, and not sure of the sanity of this course of action. The third, the large man with the shotgun, was also nervous, but he kept his own counsel, looking from the brother of Maura Tol to the smaller man.

Arise! Survive! the beast roared within him.

I'm too tired, the man answered. Unconsciousness dragged at him. *So very tired...*

The brother of Maura Tol, holding the bone spear, continued to speak, his voice a low and steady drone. "In this place where the First Hunter and the Last Defender fell, we will lay this creature who is both Elder and Shifter to rest. With his death, let the Age of the Predator end. We will bring forth the Age of Man!"

Something strange was happening to the room, and to the man, as he spoke. A sense like the heaviness of a coming thunderstorm was filling the air, charging it. To Kaiden it smelled odd and unnatural, and the beast whined uneasily. The eyes of the man standing over him dilated, glittering with light, and a golden glow suffused his flesh.

"Magic!" the second man gasped, stepping back.

"Easy, Reynolds," the large man with the shotgun warned in a deep voice.

Inside Kaiden, the Abomination snarled. There had always been rumors that the oldest of the Elders had mastered the Dark Arts, but no Shifter had ever seen them.

"B-But... It can't be!" The man staggered back from his fellow, who rounded on him, green eyes burning.

"Of course magic!" he yelled, his voice taking on echoes it didn't have before. "How do you think the humans hunted the Shifters so long ago? How do you think the Elders came to be?" He laughed, and it was as if the dark places of the universe were laughing through him.

"They're-they're a virus! A mutated virus!" Reynolds babbled, trying to believe, *willing* himself to believe.

"One thing can be Many, and the Many can be one." The man's voice boomed, like the roar of a tide. "You live in an age of vampires and werewolves and a perpetually dark sky, and you don't believe in magic?" When he chuckled, he didn't sound like a man at all.

Arise! Fight! Kill! the beast snarled. It understood, in an animal way, what this was. The man—the relative of Maura Tol—was a predator. And he had made himself something terrible.

"No, Thomas, I thought this was a message we were going to send to them all, not whatever this is," the angered Reynolds spat. "It ain't natural!"

"Hey!" the shotgun-wielder said angrily, stepping forward.

"*Natural!*" Thomas Tol scoffed, a hand lashing out with inhuman speed, fingers blurring with blue and grey light as he slapped his aide solidly across the face.

Maybe it was the ancient power of the place that gave Thomas strength, or maybe it was the fact that one hand was holding one of the ancient Shifter weapons. Or perhaps Tol was a more powerful magician than he gave himself credit for. Whatever the reason, there was a resounding crack as the aide's neck broke with the slap and his jaw cracked, blood spraying outward.

He was dead by the time he hit the floor. Blood splattered across Kaiden's body, his face, his lips. The last of the human sank into the ravening hunger of the beast.

Kaiden arched on the table, muscles rippling and bones popping, talons erupting from his hands. His mouth became a snub-nosed muzzle full of razor-sharp teeth. From overhead he heard a gasp and a shout of alarm, but he paid them no heed. He was the beast; he knew nothing but blood and slaughter.

With a roar Kaiden batted the bone spear out of the magician's hand, reflexes responding faster than they ever could have had *he* been in control of them. But the virus ruled, and it did what it had to do.

The second man, alarmed, was raising the shotgun as Thomas fell back under the onslaught. One of the wings tearing its way out of Kaiden's already-damaged back batted him across the face before a clawed hand seized him, dragging him into the reach of Kaiden's fanged snout. He tore a gobbet of flesh from the man's cheek and brow, his mouth filling with the taste of iron. He dropped the still-screaming guard and spun around to confront the more dangerous enemy: Thomas Tol.

Tol was shocked by the sudden transformation in his would-be sacrifice, but not shocked still. Under the surprise, there was hunger on his face. He slammed his two fists together in front of him and a wave of blue force buffeted Kaiden back, burning where it touched his skin. Kaiden fell back off the slab of the Tomb, the body of Reynolds crunching under his feet.

Magic, the beast sneered. *Old wolf tricks.*

The guard was still screaming. Tol was reaching for the bone spear when Kaiden leapt over the altar once again, opening his wings as much as he could in the confined space to give himself some lift. Claws raked down the magician's shoulder and outstretched arm.

Tol cried out in pain. He spun, a hand blurring blue and white to parry Kaiden's next strike. Skin sizzled where he touched. Kaiden lashed out with a boot only to find that Tol had jumped backwards, followed by blue and white negatives of himself. Blood dripped down one of Tol's arms.

The beast inside Kaiden rushed forward, focused on nothing but that trickle of thick, red liquid.

Tol slammed his fists together once more, one foot stomping against the stone. There was a loud, rumbling crack and the bubble of negative light hit Kaiden in the chest, throwing him back against the far wall as the ground started to shake.

"You're strong, Abomination," Kaiden heard Tol say. "But you're still just an animal."

Someone screamed. The scent of blood blossomed. Kaiden, his senses overwhelmed with the reek of iron, flipped back to his feet as the man who had held the shotgun staggered toward him. Tol had struck him a blow across the back, sending him stumbling toward Kaiden with blood dripping down his shoulders.

If Kaiden hadn't been so near death, or had he fed at all since the first day of his journey, he might have been able to resist the call. Drained as he was, it was too much for him. The virus had control.

Kaiden fell upon the man and tore him apart.

Chapter 30

"From the 33rd Convocation of the Order, to all aspirants, apprentices, and sorcerers: The Order is hereby disbanded. All aspirants, apprentices, and sorcerers are advised to case all magical activity immediately. Our enemies- [Here the paper is stained and illegible]
Walk in wisdom. Look to the stars, and may they shine someday upon our future meeting. We will yet bring this world back to the Light!"
−scrap of paper found in a Boston museum, dated to the late nineteenth century. (Upheld by some as conclusive proof of mortal magic users.)

Survive! Flee! Hide!
The last instincts of the beast hidden in Kaiden's blood vanished, leaving the human faculties fully in control in a world about to come down around Kaiden's ears.

What? Where? How? Kaiden ached everywhere, but the agony of unhealed gunshot wounds was gone and he was himself again. He was covered in gore, and the bodies of Reynolds and the man with the shotgun lay torn apart around him. He didn't know how long he had been lost in the frenzy, but he guessed that it could only have been minutes.

The room was still shaking, and there were hairline cracks spreading up the walls. Dust drifted down from above. Stone ground against stone.

Thomas Tol! Kaiden remembered. *The magician! He did something, used some unknown power...*

The ground shook once again as Kaiden tried to get to his feet. He felt much stronger, but full healing would take days. He seized an abandoned flashlight and turned back to the slab.

It had cracked down the center and fallen away to the sides. In the hollowed-out pit beneath lay a skeleton.

Even though every sense was telling Kaiden to flee, his feet drew him closer to the broken Tomb. He had to see. He had to *know*.

The skeleton within was tall, the shoulders broad for a human, but the skull... Kaiden's breath caught. The cheekbones arced outward, and long canines protruded from a jaw more like a canine's than a human's.

But not entirely canine. There was something about the shortened snout and underslung jaw that was distinctly bat-like. Had the First Hunter been something like what he was?

Something cracked sharply overhead, and the walls shook once more. *No time.* Kaiden caught up the bone spear that Thomas Tol hadn't been able to recover and ran.

There was only one way out that he knew, and that was back to the river. He didn't know where Tol had gone. Had he followed the trail Kaiden ran down, or had he escaped somehow through some hidden passage? There was no time to ponder the question. His feet pounded against stone, and up ahead he heard the fast-flowing river.

Upstream. Kaiden yanked off his belt and secured the spear against his back. Just having it so close to him made him feel different, somehow stronger. He launched himself into the ice-cold water.

Holding the flashlight in his teeth he swam vigorously, but the current was strong and he didn't make it far before he had to clamber onto a narrow ledge on the far side. He panted with the exertion, but his recent feeding had flushed his body with new strength.

Making certain that the spear was secure between his shoulder blades Kaiden summoned his anger and allowed his wings to sprout, claws emerging from his hands. The details of the rock around him jumped into sharp relief, newly visible to his enhanced senses. He heard again the grinding of the rock, the walls of the ravine threatening to close in.

Snarling, Kaiden leapt, opening his wings to give himself a lift as he drove his claws into the wall and pushed off once more, and then again. Each bounding pounce took him further up the ravine wall, back toward the passageway at the top and the opening he had so recently fallen through.

Finally, with aching shoulders, he reached the top, where the spiked ball still hung from the ceiling. He growled at it as he hauled himself onto the stone and ran past it, through the round room on the other side.

Darts hissed out of the wall, but he wrapped his heavy wings around himself and they didn't even break his skin. He barreled past the statues and down the juddering passage beyond. Up ahead was the pit trap, and he didn't even stop to think before leaping it and bounding up the ramp. The scent of green earth and growing things grew stronger. Silver moonlight splashed across the threshold up ahead.

Kaiden threw himself past the stone lintel and out into the clearing beyond, sucking in lungsful of fresh night air. He didn't know whether it was the same night or a different one. He supposed it didn't matter. He stood, panting and gasping, in front of the Tomb, exultant and furious.

Maura Tol, the Cat-Shifter. She set me up. She'd been working with her brother the magician. For what? Kaiden tried to puzzle it through. *For the bone spear?* Kaiden nodded his head, imagining how they must have planned it. Thomas would intercept Kaiden and kill him, far from any eyes that might see and report back, and then he would deliver the spear to his sister. With control over the East Coast Tribe, the siblings would work toward their true goal: ridding the world of Elders, and any Shifter who opposed them.

They wanted to be the top of the food chain, and they'd betray anyone they had to in order to make it there.

Howls rose from the wild valley around Kaiden, not frightening him this time but filling the Abomination with a savage joy. He stretched out his wings, luxuriating in their reach and power as he reveled in his own predatory nature.

The wolves would come to kill the trespasser in their territory. Kaiden didn't care. There were still a few hours of the night left, and he had a long way to go.

With a bound and a mighty downward sweep of his wings, Kaiden sprang into the air and shot off northward across the trees. Back toward the Great Eastern Gathering and back to where, no doubt, Maura Tol was trying to undermine him.

But I have something that you don't, don't I? Kaiden thought as he flew, a dark shadow against dark skies, the bone spear snug against his spine. *Let us see who the* true *apex predator is!*

He threw his head back and howled into the night.

Chapter 31

"Your only true ally is the sun. A twelve-gauge shotgun will sure help, but when all
your bullets are spent, look to the morning."
–mortal human adage

"Fall back! Back to the park!" Tay shouted to the last remaining Servitor guards and Elders who were still, amazingly, loyal to her.

The night was lit with flames and the occasional bullet was flying from either side, but neither side, it seemed, was too worried about the other. Both were focused on the swarm of bats that had caused so much destruction.

We must have killed it. We must have! What could have survived all of that Hellfire? But despite her own reassurances, Tay had a sneaking suspicion that Phibe was right. Somehow, the Killer had survived the chemical incendiaries her drones had fired at the bridge.

A stake to the heart, Tay thought. She felt, with no way to explain why, that the creature would have to be killed by some traditional means. Bullets and missiles and grenades were too modern, not appropriate to deal with it. *And what about the rest of The Archonate?* How on Earth was she going to fend them off?

Are they already here? When will they arrive? How do they travel? Where from?

Too many questions and never enough time to get the answers. Tay hated the questions, troublesome and never-ending. She wanted to be free of this mess, free of the killing, free from the city.

Light flickered in a window above her. Tay's gaze snapped upward, the muzzle of her gun lifting to follow. And then she froze. The movement hadn't been an attack; it was a mortal woman, looking down in fear at the street below. They stared at each other for a moment before the woman closed the shutters on the window and turned out the light, obviously afraid.

There are people here. People who need me. "Phibe?" she asked suddenly, watching as one Servitor in the flood of them ahead supported a wounded companion. Tay meant to create a clear kill zone between her people and Manhattan, and with the bridge down she had time to reconcentrate her forces and resupply where they needed it.

"Archon?" Phibe replied, her expression still tight with pain from earlier injuries.

"What would The Archonate do if they took over the city?"

"*When* they take over the city, you mean," Phibe replied.

Tay rolled her eyes. She was growing used to Phibe's morose cynicism. "To the people, I mean. Not to me."

"Honestly, Archon, I could not say. The Archonate have not been seen in person since the Renaissance, but they were famed then for their cruel games and their love of blood sports."

"Jeremiah and his culls would have pleased them, then," Tay huffed.

"Perhaps. There was something of the old cruelty to Jeremiah," Phibe said. "But at his core he was a weak man playing at strength. He would have crossed them, and they would have crushed him." She turned to look at Tay, her dark eyes hard. "You must remember that The Archonate are supposed to be ancient. There is rumor that one or two of their number were taught their cruelty in the amphitheaters of Rome, or amid the war band of Genghis Khan. They have seen it all, Archon, and they think nothing of playing games with Elders and mortals alike."

"So they won't rule fairly, then," Tay said.

"Fairly?" Phibe laughed sharply. "If they're truly coming here, if they have taken an interest in you and this city, Archon Maslov, then this continent should prepare itself for a darkness such as has not been seen since the late Middle Ages."

"Crusades," Anya said, speaking for the first time since their conversation had begun. "Witch trials."

"Purges, plagues, public executions..." Phibe said. "We have been blessed in modern times. The Archonate grew old and they slumbered. If they are awake now and—night forbid—*excited*, it will be hell on earth. Only the cruelest and the strongest will survive."

"We have technology they cannot understand," Tay said, searching for anything that might offer hope in the face of Phibe's bleak predictions. "Our science has progressed far past anything they might have imagined."

Phibe's eyes narrowed. "Perhaps that will help you." She looked back at the burning and broken bridge. "Your powers of destruction are patently unbelievable. But they have a great deal more experience in starting and winning wars than you do, young Archon."

We'll see. Tay grimaced. *We'll see about that.*

They emerged into the park, where the remaining bridge forces were gathering, fearfully looking to the sky. Blood bags were being handed out by a contingent of white-clad Servitors, and Tay took some for herself and Phibe, waving Anya forward to let her claim a bag as well. To her pleased surprise, she saw Chief Servitor Matthias, flanked by guards, making his way toward her.

"Archon." Matthias fell to one knee, head bowed. "With communications down, I thought it best to come here in person. I must apologize for my abhorrent failure to defend your District." She heard him swallow. "I offer my life as recompense."

"Don't be melodramatic, Matthias," Tay said, unthinking. "You didn't fail me; I failed this city."

A ripple of amazement went through the Servitors around her. Phibe's lips pressed into a thin line. Anya, though, looked neither surprised nor upset.

I know an Archon is supposed to be tough and aloof, but times have to change. Times have *changed, whether these people like it or not,* Tay thought, breathing deeply.

"Yes. An Archon apologizing. Stranger things, hmm?" She laughed, and the nearest Servitors looked alarmed by her apparent conviviality. They were used to dealing with a treacherous, dangerous leader, not an ally.

"Archon?" Phibe urged.

"Enough!" Tay snapped, putting a little of the warning growl back into her tone. The Servitors snapped to attention around them. "Times have changed, and I am not Jeremiah," she said to all who were gathered there—all of the Elders, the Servitors, even the few mortals who had wandered, bravely, from their tenements. "I am Tabitha Maslov, Archon of Brooklyn, and we are facing an enemy the likes of which the city has never seen before!"

Her voice rang out over the assembled crowd. "Our enemy isn't Bethania, or any of the other Archons in New York. It is The Archonate itself, with its lapdog creature, the Dark Moon Killer!"

There was a range of moans and worried gasps from the defenders, as well as an almost inaudible groan of despair from Phibe behind her.

"However, my people, we have one strength that our enemies don't!" Tay shouted. "We *know* this District, this city, these people. We *know* this time. All of our enemies are living in the past, in a fantasy land of their own making. They want to go on as though this is the nineteenth century, or the eighteenth, or the bloody European Renaissance! *Not us!*" She raised a fist and bared her fangs.

"*We* are moderns. We have the technology and we know how to use it. We are not clinging to some archaic view of strength or battle or strategy. We will adapt and move with our times in order to defend this District from all invaders!"

A few scattered cheers went up from the defenders. *They have to believe in me,* Tay thought. *They have to believe in something to follow, and*

since I can't sell them the traditional image of the cruel, all-powerful vam-
pire overlord, I'll give them something new: the young and inspired, the
Archon who will lead them into a brighter, brand new age.

Tay's gaze swept over the crowd, finding the eyes of those who believed her, those who placed their trust in their Archon. "Things will
have to change, my friends. We cannot live in the Predatory society of
yesterday.

"We have set ourselves up as overlords, believed ourselves to be better, stronger, faster. But the enemy we face now is stronger than any one
Elder, and they will not care that we have the virus in common. They
will subjugate vampires as easily as mortals. If we are to fight them, we
must fight *together.*"

There were no cheers. Whispers ran through the assembled citizens
of Brooklyn.

"She's right!" Anya said, pitching her voice to be heard over the
murmurs and the shifting of the crowd. "However strong any of you
may be—however fierce in a fight—you saw what that creature was capable of. The Archonate it serves is just as powerful. We cannot stop
them unless we trust in our Archon. Trust in *each other* and fight as
one!"

"So what do we do?" someone in the crowd called out.

"This entire front row of buildings needs to be cleared of occu-
pants," Tay ordered. "Mortals, Blood Dolls, whomever is living there.
They are to be left *unharmed* and escorted to somewhere safe from im-
mediate attack." Tay pointed to the buildings between the park and the
river.

"There are more of them than there are of us, and so when they
come we want to give them as hard a time as possible! They must not
take a building without the fear that there will be a sniper inside, or
a maze, or a trap. Let our enemies know that if they choose to take
Brooklyn, they will have to do it street by street! House by house!
Fighter by fighter!"

The cheers that followed actually sounded like the crowd meant them.

Chapter 32

"The fact of the matter is that we do not truly know the limits of the virus. Certainly, there are ways to kill an Elder, but as the strength of the virus and its hold on the host increases the methods by which the host can be dispatched seem to require greater and more concentrated effort. In a sufficiently advanced subject,
true immortality might indeed be possible."
–from the notes of M. Shelley, M.D., Ph.D. (BANNED, PRIVATE COLLECTION)

The night was past its halfway point, and the hive of activity in the park had died down to a watchful, expectant hush. There were camps, rough shelters, and barricades thrown up, rifles and ammunition stacked behind them. Tay saw that some Elder had come up with the idea of parking Blood Bank transport vans at the rear entrance to the park. From there, a steady supply of the District's dwindling blood resources could be handed out to those who required them.

With a shiver, Tay thought that they looked a little bit like the burger vans that could sometimes be seen outside mortal clubs. She tried to ignore the growling hunger in her veins.

Now and again there was a shout or a scream, or the occasional blast of gunfire, but considering that they were at war the night was surprisingly quiet. At about four in the morning, Tay left Matthias working on the defenses in order to head back out with Phibe so they could scout the bridge and survey what was happening. She had left Anya in charge of organizing supplies.

The street they ran down was quiet—deserted—and there were only a few lights left on in the buildings. Her Servitors had cleared them, despite some resistance from the frightened and confused mortals within.

I'm a terrible leader. People will never forgive me for what I'm doing.

By the time they reached the far end of the street and looked out over the oily water and the blackened ruins of the bridge, Tay amended her judgement to *what I've done.*

The bridge was a wreck of burnt brick and twisted metal. Tay scanned its still-smoking surface, wondering if she could see movement and whether the noises she heard were just the hisses and pops of metal cooling.

"She won't attack tonight," Phibe whispered next to her. "She'll need to either take the bridge to the north of here or get boats, all of which will take time."

"Time that we need," Tay said meaningfully.

Phibe turned to look at her in astonishment. "You still think you can win this, don't you?"

Tay opened her mouth, ready to respond with an unequivocal 'yes', but then paused as she considered the enormity of what faced them all. Instead, when she next spoke it was to say, "I have to."

"The Archonate may not need the same resources," Phibe said. She gave Tay a searching look. "I was against your Shifter allies initially, but we could do with some strong bodies right now."

Don't I know it. Tay almost groaned. There had been no word from Kaiden. No word from the Gathering. She had no idea if the other Shifters had simply rejected his plans, or if they had torn him to pieces. She might never know.

That goodbye might have been the last time I'll ever see him.

A blood-curdling scream split the night. Tay startled, eyes searching the darkness desperately for the source. *There.* "The old hospital."

Phibe reached for her radio. "Chief? Did you hear that? Yes. The old hospital. Send a team over. The Archon and I— Well, we are going in, it looks like." There was a hiss of static and a half-audible answer from the other side. "No. I do not think I can stop her. Out."

Phibe's opinion of Tay's rash decision was clear on her face. Tay paid it no mind. Cursing, the other woman followed her over the fence and toward the smashed windows of the abandoned medical building.

When it had been functioning, many decades ago, the Brooklyn River Hospital had been little more than a city clinic. About the size of a primary school it had only a handful of floors, and wasn't large enough to get lost in. Tay had a dim recollection that it had last been used as some kind of retirement home before it was finally decommissioned under Archon Jeremiah (there wasn't any money in keeping sick mortals alive if they couldn't produce good blood).

That was another thing that made Tay's claws itch when she thought about her predecessor.

"Archon?" Phibe slid in through the window behind her and landed lightly on the floor of the day room where Tay stood. Chairs and tables were broken, lying on their sides on the floor. A small nurses' station, long since ransacked, sat to one side. Ahead, a door opened on the main corridor that ran the length of the ground floor.

A body hit the floor at the end of the corridor. For a flicker of an instant Tay thought it had fallen from the ceiling, and then she realized that there was a stairwell hidden opposite. The smell of fresh mortal blood filled her senses and a snarl rose in her throat.

"Get away! Get out! Get—" The shouting burst into the corridor as a figure, a woman, launched herself after the body. She rolled as she hit the floor, clutching a shotgun, and turned to fire both barrels back up the stairs. Sobs wracked through her.

Get up! Get running! Tay thought, sprinting for the end of the corridor with Phibe on her heels.

"Archon!" Phibe yelled. "Careful!"

The woman dropped a box of cartridges, shells scattering across the floor, her hands shaking too badly to load the gun. A shadow fell over her and a despairing wail burst from her throat.

Tay was almost there, her vampiric speed eating up the distance in a flash. The distraught woman in front of her was the mortal equivalent, Tay thought, of a Feral. She clearly had no money and her clothes were torn and ragged, her hair dirty and tousled. Tay imagined that she and the dead one had probably hidden out in the hospital, attempting to avoid the attention of the Elders.

I might be like you, if our lives had been different, Tay thought as she dropped to one knee to get a view up the stairwell, sliding on the worn linoleum. She raised her gun.

It had to be Bethania's people. *Or one of my own Elders, gone rogue.* But it was neither. A thousand tiny bodies whirled down the stairs, coalescing into a column before her eyes, solidifying into a humanoid shape.

Tay fired, knocking small showers of furry bodies from the main host in little puffs of screaming blood and bat wing.

"It's the Killer!" Tay shouted, expending her magazine and grabbing the woman by the shoulders. Her gunfire had slowed down the creature's re-formation by seconds. "Get up!" she shouted to the mortal woman. "RUN!" She threw some measure of her power into it, injecting her voice with the growl of a predator, forcing the woman to hear and obey. Humans had so little control of their instincts.

The woman scrambled to her feet and fled.

"Here!" Phibe shouted, heaving open a set of double doors to reveal a service elevator. A light still blinked over the control panel. In a panicked rush, Tay and the homeless woman jumped into the elevator. Phibe followed, hitting the call button for the top floor.

There was a grinding noise, but nothing happened. Tay's stomach dropped. *We've put ourselves in a metal box with no way out.*

A sound like nails on a chalkboard, sharp and unpleasant. It took Tay a moment to realize that it was the creature laughing. The sound of it echoed down the stairwell and rang in her ears.

The Dark Moon Killer stepped off the staircase, his fine leather boots making no sound on the dusty floor of the hospital.

He looked different, Tay thought. Bits of his cloak and the flesh beneath were ragged and tattered. He moved stiffly. *Did I hurt him when I shot him? Was it the napalm?*

With a cheery ding, the doors of the elevator began to close. The Killer, still laughing as though it was all a joke, came down the hall toward them. In the reflected light from the streetlamps outside, Tay saw that half his face was charred and sagging, and half-melted.

So he can be hurt after all! The doors closed, and there was a jolt as the elevator started to slowly shudder upwards.

"Did you see that?" Tay breathed excitedly.

"I saw," Phibe said, voice low.

"He's injured. We can kill him!" Relief rushed through her.

"Who?" the mortal woman asked. She was about Tay's height, dirty blonde hair pulled back into a loose ponytail, her face smeared with blood and dirt. Phibe didn't acknowledge her.

"The creature that attacked you," Tay answered, as kindly as she could. "Do you know who I am?"

"Y-You're an Elder, Ma'am." The woman bowed her head. "We didn't mean any insult, Farouk and I, we just came in here to-to..." She shivered, terrified.

Phibe's lip curled in disgust at the display of abject fear.

"It's okay. We've not come here to hurt you," Tay said. "I'm your Archon. Your *new* Archon. My name's Tabitha."

"R-R-Rose." The woman's eyes were wide, her voice barely audible.

"That Killer, why did he attack you? When?" Tay asked as the elevator shuddered and creaked toward the upper floors.

"Ju-Just a second ago. Farouk was looking at the fire on the bridge and it just— it just came out of nowhere."

"The most innocent," Phibe said, referring to the Killer's particular taste for killing those who had the least to do with its primary victim.

Or maybe he knows exactly who to kill, Tay thought bitterly. *Those I seek to protect. What did he say? That I would see all that I love and hold dear torn apart? He can't get to Kaiden. What other stance have I taken, except to protect the mortals?*

There was a grinding, tearing noise from below. Rose screamed. Tay exchanged a glance with Phibe. Metal shrieked, tortured, as it was pulled aside. The symbol for the third floor lit up.

"He's forced his way into the elevator shaft," Phibe hissed. A dark laugh echoed from below.

"The trapdoor!" Tay pointed to a service opening at the top of the elevator car. She leapt up, slamming the heel of her hand into it with enough force to dent the metal. The elevator rocked beneath her as she landed on the thin, moldy carpet. Her second strike burst the trapdoor open to reveal a slowly approaching ceiling and the mechanical winches and works of the hoist system.

Tay was the first up onto the top of the car as, far below them, the sound of screeching and twittering filled the space. The Killer was shifting his form. In a moment, he would be able to follow. "Hurry!" Tay shouted, reaching down with one hand to life Rose none-too-gently through the opening. Phibe followed easily.

Below them, Tay heard the noise of a thousand tiny bodies slamming themselves into the underside of the lift. If it caught up with them... Tay didn't have time to worry about it. She shoved Rose onto one of the stabilizing cables, loading the human's shotgun with rapid hands and pointing it at the link between the winch and her feet.

Bats began to swarm through the narrow space between the elevator and the walls. Phibe hissed a curse and Tay fired.

In the closed space, the sound was deafening. The elevator beneath their feet lurched as its connection to the first support gave way. But the bats were everywhere, clambering over each other to reach them, and the cables still held. Were the rest clinging to the underside of the elevator car? Tay imagined them there, a coalescing ball of fury and hatred. All that weight, pulling on the weakened winch.

"Go!" Tay shouted at Phibe, loading the shotgun again. "Get her up to the roof!"

Phibe leapt for the cables, wrapping an arm around the still-screaming human and beginning to haul them both toward the maintenance hatch overhead. Tay took aim at another anchor point and fired again.

The sound of metal snapping was clear and sharp. Tay flung herself upward as the elevator plummeted, taking the clutching swarm of killer bats with it. Her hand curled around a cable and closed tight. For an instant she lingered, watching the elevator car rattle downward, throwing up sparks where its edges hit the walls. A few disoriented bats fluttered weakly around her, and she swatted them aside with the barrel of the shotgun.

The elevator crashed through the ground floor and into the basement, sending up a plume of ash and dust.

I've shot it, Tay thought as she began climbing after Phibe and Rose. *I've fired napalm at it, and now I've dropped an elevator on it. When will this thing die?*

Never, a cynical part of her replied. *Never.*

Chapter 33

"When death comes, meet it with bared fang."
–Elder proverb, often attributed to Archon Zyanya of Queens

Tay, Phibe, and the mortal scrambled out onto the roof. The city, sprawling around them, was eerily silent. It didn't seem right, after their terrifying ordeal, that the world had not somehow changed. Rose collapsed, coughing dust out of her lungs as the two vampires searched for an escape route.

"It's a hit and run predator," Tay said. "It may not even come after us..."

"You are right. It may find someone else to eat," Phibe replied.

"Or it might not," Rose said from where she lay, her voice thin. The two vampires turned to see what the mortal pointed at.

There, coming toward them above the city skyline, was a black cloud. It was dark smoke, curling around a mass of chittering, screaming bodies. If the Dark Moon Killer's swarm was impressive, this looked like doomsday. It was easily five or six times the size of the Dark Moon swarm, and as it approached Brooklyn Tay's stomach twisted.

"The Archonate!" Phibe breathed, and in an instant Tay knew that she was right.

"Wh-What do we do?" Rose gasped.

"There's nothing to do," Tay replied. "We fight."

"We die," Phibe concluded as, with a mighty hissing roar, the windows on the ground floor of the hospital burst and the Dark Moon swarm poured onto the roof.

I'll keep my eyes open. Tay gritted her teeth, waiting to feel at any moment the bites of a thousand bats' teeth, but they never came. Instead, the swarm started to coalesce into a tighter and tighter knot before her, reforming as the Killer. Or what was left of it.

The Killer still stood tall, but burns and tears marred the ghostly white of his skin and he moved with a stiffness that hadn't been present before. His long cloak hung in ragged tatters.

How much does it take to form and reform as the bats? Is he losing more of himself, even now? Tay's thoughts raced as the black cloud of The Archonate drew nearer to the river.

"Have you had enough yet?" Tay called out to the Dark Moon Killer. "Maybe the modern age isn't really the time for you!"

The Killer hissed and twitched, and then in a blur of movement was standing directly in front of Tay. Its taloned hand snapped out and backhanded her hard enough to send her sprawling onto the gritty hospital rooftop.

"Impudent whelp!" the Killer coughed, its ruined and battered face a rictus of fury. "You have no idea what is coming! My masters, the Rulers of the Night, arrive before you even now. You. Will. *Bow.*"

There was a bang of muzzle fire, coming this time not from Tay or Phibe or Rose, but from a set of figures leaping over the edge of the roof: burly Servitors in heavy combat gear. At their center, holding a smoking pistol, was a dark-haired woman clad in leather. Disks of gold set with polished turquoise dangled from her ears.

"Whatever happens," she said, voice a low growl, "you will not be there to see it."

Her Servitor bodyguards opened fire, pummeling the Dark Moon Killer, and he shrieked in pain and anger as he was driven backward.

"Archon Zyanya?" Tay gasped incredulously.

"The very same," the tall woman said. There was a faint, lilting accent to the words, as though English wasn't her first language. "I've heard a great deal about you, Archon Maslov."

Tay had never even gotten around to writing the letter she'd intended to send the Archon of Queens. The Dark Moon Killer's arrival and

Bethania's stunt on the bridge had put an abrupt end to her war council. "Most of it bad, I assume," Tay said as Zyanya's Servitors brightened the night with muzzle flare.

Archon Zyanya laughed. "Most of it," she agreed. "Though not all. But you are the one here fighting while the others prepare to grovel before The Archonate, and so here I am, too. Queens is *mine*, and not even the demon lords of old will take it from me."

The Dark Moon Killer snarled, bursting into a cloud of bats and spiraling upward.

Tay swore. "How are we supposed to defend against that?"

"You are so young," Archon Zyanya said. Her lips curled into a savage grin as, behind her, her Servitors exchanged their weapons for nozzles attached to packs on their backs. "*This* is how you deal with the oldest ones, little Archon Maslov. Watch and learn."

One by one, the Servitors around her raised the hoses in their hands and pulled the triggers. Arcs of fire plumed into the night, and the swarm screamed almost as one.

"Zyanya!" The appalled shout came from their right and Tay spun to see Bethania gaining the roof, accompanied by her own set of bodyguards and a pair of Elders Tay recognized as Jackson and Gatsby. Bethania, to Tay's surprise, wore a pair of high-waisted pants and a collared blouse instead of her usual slip dress. "What are you doing?"

"What does it look like?" the Archon Zyanya retorted.

"Archon?" It was Phibe, sidling back toward her and leaning in close to speak softly. "We need to leave. You must gather your forces." The older vampire was looking uncertainly between the other two Archons, her expression tight. Rose, the mortal Tay had nearly forgotten, was edging toward the door that led back down into the hospital.

"Oh, no you don't!" Bethania snapped, swiveling on one elegantly pointed shoe to level her gun at Phibe and Tay. "I came here to make a deal, and you're my bargaining chip."

"You're a fool if you think they won't take Manhattan, Bethania," Archon Zyanya said coldly over the shrieks of the flaming bats. "Bargaining chip or not."

Tay jumped in to follow her lead. "Bethania, join us! Stand with Brooklyn and Queens against The Archonate."

"Are you insane?" Bethania laughed, the sound no longer light and silver but ragged. "None of us will last against The Archonate." Her gaze flicked toward the leather-clad Archon of Queens. "Not even you, Zyanya."

She turned back to Tay. "Resign your hold over Brooklyn, hand over your District to me, and perhaps The Archonate will spare some of your people."

Fire still roared into the sky, bright against the dark sky and the approaching cloud of The Archonate swarm.

"I have never begged, and I will not start now," Zyanya hissed. "Are you predator or prey, Bethania?"

"Tabitha," Phibe said, voice low and warning.

Tay screwed her eyes shut, trying to think. *There has to be a way out of this!*

She didn't want to give control of the city to Bethania, but even with Zyanya's aid they couldn't stand against The Archonate. If Bethania could make a deal, would it save the lives of those who had followed Tay to disaster?

"*Archon!*" Phibe snarled at Tay. "You realize that Bethania will hand you—and all of your closest allies with you—over to The Archonate, do you not? They will want your head!"

I know. Tay hissed in animal frustration and opened her eyes. "I know, Phibe. And it isn't fair to you, but I have to save the city. If I give myself up maybe they'll leave the rest of New York alone, and if it costs my life..."

Behind them, what remained of the Dark Moon Killer had finally found a gap in the covering fire. It swarmed through, diving at the defenders.

Chapter 34

"The Dark Moon Killer is not the only monster that stalks Elder legend. Certainly, it is one of the most mysterious, but there are tales of other creatures just as dreadful: ancient and powerful vampires gone mad, sorcerers with the power to strip the very marrow from a man's bones, and great hunters who stalked our kind nearly to extinction in the New World. But most of these are old horrors, long ago forgotten."
–excerpt from *On Black Wings Rising: The Origins of the Dark Moon Killer*, by Valentine Clark

Bethania was screaming. Tay heard a cry of alarm she thought might be Gatsby's, and a snarl from Zyanya. The Dark Moon swarm was far smaller than it had been, now no more than a few hundred bats weaving and diving across the rooftop, but that was enough. Something latched on to Tay's cheek, sending a sharp spike of agony through her. She clawed the body aside, crushing it easily with one hand as another latched on to her jacket.

The Servitors were not so lucky. They had only very limited healing ability, and no natural resistance to the Dark Moon Killer's attack. The sound of their desperate screams turned Tay's stomach.

"Down!" Phibe was shouting. "Stay *down*, Archon!"

Tay dropped and felt the roar of fire close overhead as one of the Servitors, spinning in an attempt to fight off the bats, turned his flamethrower their way.

Were there more bats than there had been a moment before?

The noise of wings eddied and faded, replaced by the thud of Servitor bodies, half eviscerated, hitting the grit and asphalt of the hospital roof. The guards were dead, and the Archons and their accomplices were all that stood before the gathering storm of The Archonate.

It's over. All over. I failed. Tay wept tears of blood as the bats whirled together and the Dark Moon Killer coalesced into its material form. She wished Kaiden was there at her side. Wished she could have seen him one last time before it all ended.

No, something deep in her snarled. *Not like this.* It couldn't be over. *"Are you predator or prey?"* she remembered Zyanya asking. *Maybe at least I can kill it.* Tay staggered to her feet, reaching for a weapon. Her hand closed around the hilt of her knife.

Bethania, in her pearls and her heels, was writhing in agony on the asphalt, her blouse stained with blood; the thin fabric had done little to protect her. Jackson and Gatsby, with wounds of their own, crouched over her. It seemed her loyalty to The Archonate hadn't spared her; maybe the creature had just been too ravenous to care. Zyanya was bleeding from a pair of gashes opened in her cheek, but seemed otherwise untouched. Phibe crouched, snarling, between Zyanya and Tay, her eyes fixed on the creature opposite them.

Despite his recent feeding, the Dark Moon Killer was just a shred of what it had been. Its skin was burnt black, sloughing off its bones. The billowing cloak was gone entirely. It steamed as it staggered forward, looking more like some ghoulish mummy from a nightmare than like any kind of Elder.

"You think you can stop the storm that is coming?" The Killer raised its arms, indicating the dark smoke overhead, the hundred-thousand vampire bats swirling within it. The air was filled with their angered shrieks, the thunder of their combined wing beats.

At the Killer's feet, Tay saw a lump of dirty-blonde hair. *Rose, the mortal.* She hadn't made it to the door. She was dead, eaten alive by the swarm.

And he's walking over her body as if she never even existed. Somehow, this simple act of thoughtless degradation enraged Tay more than anything else had. She bared her fangs, raised her knife, and charged at the monstrous thing.

The Killer was slower than it had been, but it still managed to latch one set of blackened talons around her wrist. It yanked, pulling her off balance. Tay let herself fall and, as she did, drove her knife downward. She thought of The Archonate, directing this creature, and screamed with rage and hate. Rage not just against them, but against every Elder who had ever murdered a mortal without a second thought, hatred for the Predatory Society itself... Distantly, she could hear Phibe and others shouting.

She felt the knife scrape over the brittle, burnt bones of the thing's ribcage before the claws on its other hand seized her by the hair on the back of her head. With a strength that she still couldn't match it yanked her backwards, baring her neck. Fangs sank into her throat.

Tay screamed. The dark dream swirled around her, rising up to engulf her as the virus inside her body reacted to the virus inside the creature above her.

She heard a voice she thought was Jackson's shout her name. A body—*Phibe's?*—slammed into them and was thrown aside. Unconsciousness pulled at Tay, threatening to take her under as the Dark Moon Killer fed on her, restoring himself swallow by swallow.

A shape burst out of the sky, barreling *through* the descending columns of The Archonate, and swept across the rooftop towards her on dark wings.

Kaiden, she thought, abruptly struggling in the Dark Moon Killer's hold. *Kaiden. You've come at last!*

The Hybrid's hands wrenched the Killer's hold on her away. Tay staggered to one knee. Kaiden and the Dark Moon Killer hit the asphalt, tumbling across it to land with Kaiden crouched over the creature, roaring his fury.

"Archon!" Phibe was at her side, a shoulder under her arm, helping her to her feet.

Zyanya hissed something that sounded like a startled curse. Her dark eyes were fixed on Kaiden and the Dark Moon Killer, struggling against each other for dominance.

"Stop him!" Bethania shouted, apparently still willing to defend the Killer that hadn't cared to spare her. "Get that Abomination off The Archonate's servant!"

"Don't!" Tay was still weak, her voice not as strong as she would have liked it to be, but Jackson and Gatsby, already hesitant to attack Kaiden in his hulking beast form, glanced her way. "Neither of you can fight him," she warned them, leaning heavily into Phibe's support. "He'll just kill you."

"I'd take her word for it," Zyanya advised.

Kaiden snarled down into the Dark Moon Killer's face, and then he reached back and closed his clawed hand around the haft of a short, curved spear that had been strapped between his wings. It was white as bone, gleaming in the dim light, and something about it made Tay's chest tighten with an old, instinctive fear.

Bethania saw it and gasped. Jackson and Gatsby backed up, suddenly wary. Tay felt Phibe tense at her side and heard Zyanya growl.

Whatever Kaiden had intended to find in his journey to take leadership of the tribe Lubok's death had handed him, it seemed he had returned with a weapon even the Archons feared.

Will it be enough to turn the tide of this war?

Chapter 35

"Like the wolf, the Shifter loves for life. Few of us in these days, scattered and worn down as we are, find the mates we were meant to spend our days beside. If you do find that one, hold on and never let go."
–from the writings of Aila Armel, Shifter of the Bear Clan

Kaiden had flown through the night and the day, through the morning and the afternoon and the evening to get to the Great Eastern Gathering, bringing with him the bone spear of the Hunter. It hadn't taken him long to discover that Maura Tol had vanished. She must have received word from her brother of his failure to sacrifice the Abomination and retrieve the relic. Maura had been long gone by the time of his arrival, but the suspicions and accusations that she left behind had remained. In the face of them, even the bone spear hadn't entirely won the others over.

A little over a third of the Eastern packs had refused to follow Kaiden, mostly Larson and his group, and Kaiden had growled at them to leave anyway. Still, the outcome could have been worse. Those Shifters who had human relatives in the city, or near to it, had followed him, and many others had been awed by the ancient relic he displayed.

"No Alpha has ever achieved this," the Archivist had intoned, marveling at the bone spear. "This relic has hunted mammoths and saber-toothed cats. It defended our shores from the Elders. Now, once again, it is in the hand of a powerful Hunter."

Once again it will defend us, Kaiden thought as he winged toward the city, his Tribe following on foot. There was a reek of something wrong in the world ahead. Something ancient and evil. He had flown on, tirelessly, south and east, and now the skyline loomed ahead. And above it...

Kaiden didn't know what the swarm was, but he knew that it stood between him and Tay. He plunged through it, ignoring the bats that flew at him, sinking their teeth into shoulder or forearm or thigh. They behaved like no animal he had ever seen, but he had no time for that mystery. His heart pushed him onward, following a scent trail that led down to the roof of an abandoned Brooklyn hospital, where his love was in the grip of a charred, skeletal creature with its fangs buried in her throat.

Until that moment, there had been enough of the human left in Kaiden for a little rationality. Seeing her there, her head lolling back as the creature fed, a dark-skinned woman trying in vain to free her from the thing's grip, the beast within roared in fury.

Kaiden didn't stop to consider tactics or strategy. He shot downward and tore the Dark Moon Killer from his beloved's neck, wrenching it sideways. Together, they hit the ground and rolled. Claws burnt black by fire reached for Kaiden's face but Kaiden slammed the thing against the asphalt, snarling down into its ruined face. His hand snatched up the bone spear and he drove it down toward the undead thing.

The creature hissed, catching the spear in one hand and pushing back against it with immense strength, fangs bared in a rictus grin. Kaiden growled, jaws snapping less than a hand's breadth from the creature's face.

The hand on the bone spear began to shake and the burned thing uttered a strange, puzzled snarl. *Did the spear cause it some harm?* Kaiden wondered. It whipped itself around, both legs getting under Kaiden and heaving, kicking him back. It looked down at its smoking hand.

Unfurling his wings to catch the air, the Abomination lashed out with both clawed feet and feinted toward the creature's face with the bone spear. It ducked, laughing at the deceptively easy move, and its clawed hand swung for his exposed, vulnerable belly.

"Kaiden!" Tay shouted somewhere out of his line of sight.

Kaiden reversed his grip and slid the bone spear through the creature's ribs and into its shriveled and blackened heart.

The Dark Moon Killer gurgled, confusion written across what was left of its face. It had been alive for a *long* time, thousands of years maybe, and it had forgotten how to die. It looked at its chest and the black stain spreading outward from the spear in its heart, and its jaws snapped feebly on the air.

"No!" he heard a familiar voice shout. "No! Don't—!"

The Dark Moon Killer collapsed into a heap of bones and ash.

Kaiden snatched the bone spear from the mess the thing had left behind and turned to face the vampires. Tay was there. Even lost as he was to the beast, he knew her. She leaned against the side of a dark-skinned woman he didn't recognize, but the way Tay leaned on the woman said 'Pack'. Tay took a stumbling step forward and all but fell into Kaiden's arms.

He wrapped his arms around her, pulling her close, and his wings sheltered her from the world as his eyes moved over the rest of the people on the roof. There was a tall woman in leather he didn't recognize. A pair of male Elders. And, there, one he knew—the Archon Bethania, her previously flawless skin marred by a score of bite wounds still sluggishly bleeding. Bodies were scattered across the asphalt behind her. Bethania looked at Kaiden with horror.

"Kaiden," Tay said. "The Archonate—"

Her voice was drowned out by the thunder of wings and the screech of bats, and Kaiden turned just as the maelstrom of creatures overhead drew itself into columns. The smoke that wound through the swarm coiled itself together. Each column coalesced into something almost human-shaped and then, where they had been, were seven finely robed figures. Kaiden's nose picked up the scent of iron and grave dirt. His hand tightened around the haft of the spear.

The Archonate had arrived in Brooklyn.

Chapter 36

"If The Archonate exists (and I am certain that they do), their rising would be not a gift but a calamity. A danger of the greatest immediacy. For what can be left in them that is human? What do they know of mercy, or of loyalty? We may all be Elders, but to any creature so ancient those of us who have faced down only a few centuries must seem very nearly a different species."

–rom the journals of Nathaniel Lane (BANNED)

Some of the seven wore robes. Others were dressed in armor or kimonos or evening gowns. All of them had eyes that glittered darkly and sets of shining double fangs. They stood in silence, watching the scene before them with an air of cold amusement.

They smelled like Elder but also like something else, concentrated and powerful. It was as though he had spent his life thinking domestic cats were lions and then had met a lion for the first time. When they moved they did so in strange, stop-motion flickers, shadows curling lovingly around them as they seemed to jump the distance between positions without moving at all. Kaiden felt speared by the ice in their eyes, held as if mesmerized. He snarled at them, cradling Tay closer beneath his wings.

"Abomination." It was hard to tell which of them had hissed the word. The one with the Roman nose and the curling hair? The short woman with dreadlocks? The tall, slender youth with the ice-white hair and steel-gray eyes? The voice seemed to eddy and swirl between them, as if they shared it. The word was assessment, judgement, and decision all in one.

"Archons." Another word.

"You can't have her!" Kaiden snarled, words mangled by the animal shape of his mouth.

Seven heads turned as one to look his way. Silence swelled and something passed between them, a decision shared by some means the younger creatures before them couldn't understand. *How old are they?* some still-human sliver of Kaiden wondered. Was there, among them, a vampire who had seen the Crusades? A creature born before the founding of London?

"You killed him." The words swam in his thoughts, and he wondered if he was hearing them aloud at all. Were they speaking directly into his mind? *Into all our minds?* Seven pairs of eyes turned in unison to the pile of bones that had been the Dark Moon Killer.

Kaiden bared his teeth. "Leave Brooklyn, or I'll send you the same way."

Laughter, sharp and strangely echoing, made Kaiden's head swim. Tay swayed in his arms. One of the vampires behind him growled.

"Good," The Archonate said.

"Most High Masters," Bethania said, stumbling forward. "I am the Archon Bethania of Manhattan, your loyal child. I have fought the false Archon Tabitha Maslov at every step, sought to preserve your precepts in this city, and to build a District in which your legacy might be known.

"Accept, I beg you, these traitors and Abominations as your rightful due and go back to your rest."

The fur along Kaiden's ruff bristled, and he growled low in his throat. These Elders standing before them would not touch his mate. He would shred every one of them apart before he allowed it. At his side the woman Tay had been leaning against snarled, and he felt a sense of kinship in their shared anger.

Tay said nothing. Kaiden could scent the distress rolling off her, but she made no argument against Bethania. He looked down at her, wondering what had stopped his strong, proud mate from refuting the other Archon's offer to the ancient Elders.

"We know you, child," The Archonate said. *"And we know your deeds. But this is no longer about the traitor and her Abomination."* They laughed. *"Too long have we slept, letting these modern nights pass us by. For your loyalty, you may reside here in this District. Yours we shall take, along with the rest of this city."*

"You will *not!*" someone hissed and Kaiden remembered the other woman, the one in worn leather. She stepped forward. "I, too, am one of your own, but I will not grovel for what is already mine. If you want Queens, you will have to take it from me."

"Is that so?" Amusement radiated through the words.

"I will not just hand over what I've fought for," the Archon of Queens snarled.

"Very well. Keep it. For now." The words were indulgent. Not a concession, but the easy disregard of a cat toying with its kill. *"We will see what we think when we have visited. Now, though, now..."*

The voice that was many voices and one lifted, and rang out over the city like thunder. Kaiden imagined that there was not a single person in New York—Elder, Shifter, or mortal—who didn't hear the words. *"NOW, A NEW REIGN SHALL BEGIN. REJOICE, FOR THE ARCHONATE COMES TO NEW YORK CITY, AND HERE WE SHALL RULE."*

To those on the roof they added, "Brooklyn shall be given to Bethania. Zyanya holds Queens. The once-Archon Tabitha Maslov is stripped of all rank and title, but allowed to live."

"What?" Bethania protested.

"We have lived a long time. It is rare that something interests us, and we have decided this game shall be an amusing one to play!"

With a swirling roar and a noise of thousands upon thousands of wings, the seven figures dissolved into bats and mist and arced up over the city toward Manhattan. There to take residence in the capital of their new empire.

On the roof, Bethania was weeping tears of blood.

"You should count yourself lucky you survived," Tay's pack-mate said, her voice calm, "Archon Bethania."

"They are playing games with us," Bethania snarled. "We're just playthings to them."

"But we're alive," Tay said, speaking for the first time since The Archonate landed on the roof. "All of us."

Kaiden opened his wings to let her step out from between them. She was weak still, the skin drawn thin over her cheekbones, but her eyes burned with certainty. "And where there is life, there is hope."

She turned and smiled at Kaiden. "I hope you're ready for a fight."

THE END

The Queen's Alpha Series

Eternal
Everlasting
Unceasing
Evermore
Forever
Boundless
Prophecy
Protected
Foretelling
Revelation
Betrayal
Resolved

The Omega Queen Series

Discipline
Bravery
Courage
Conquer
Strength
Validation
Approval
Blessing
Balance
Grievance
Enchanted
Gratified

Find W.J. May

Website:
http://www.wjmaybooks.com
Facebook:
https://www.facebook.com/pages/Author-WJ-May-FAN-PAGE/
141170442608149
Newsletter:
SIGN UP FOR W.J. May's Newsletter to find out about new releases,
updates, cover reveals and even freebies!
http://eepurl.com/97aYf

More books by W.J. May

The Chronicles of Kerrigan

Book I - *Rae of Hope* is FREE!
Book Trailer:
http://www.youtube.com/watch?v=gILAwXxx8MU
Book II - *Dark Nebula*
Book Trailer:
http://www.youtube.com/watch?v=Ca24STi_bFM
Book III - *House of Cards*
Book IV - *Royal Tea*
Book V - *Under Fire*
Book VI - *End in Sight*
Book VII – *Hidden Darkness*
Book VIII – *Twisted Together*
Book IX – *Mark of Fate*
Book X – *Strength & Power*
Book XI – *Last One Standing*
BOOK XII – *Rae of Light*

PREQUEL –
Christmas Before the Magic

Question the Darkness
Into the Darkness
Fight the Darkness
Alone the Darkness
Lost the Darkness

SEQUEL –
Matter of Time
Time Piece
Second Chance
Glitch in Time
Our Time
Precious Time

Hidden Secrets Saga:
Download Seventh Mark part 1 For FREE
Book Trailer:
http://www.youtube.com/watch?v=Y-_vVYC1gvo
Like most teenagers, Rouge is trying to figure out who she is and what she wants to be. With little knowledge about her past, she has questions but has never tried to find the answers. Everything changes when she befriends a strangely intoxicating family. Siblings Grace and Michael, appear to have secrets which seem connected to Rouge. Her hunch is confirmed when a horrible incident occurs at an outdoor party. Rouge may be the only one who can find the answer.

An ancient journal, a Sioghra necklace and a special mark force life-altering decisions for a girl who grew up unprepared to fight for her life or others.

All secrets have a cost and Rouge's determination to find the truth can only lead to trouble...or something even more sinister.

RADIUM HALOS - THE SENSELESS SERIES
Book 1 is FREE

Everyone needs to be a hero at one point in their life.

The small town of Elliot Lake will never be the same again.

Caught in a sudden thunderstorm, Zoe, a high school senior from Elliot Lake, and five of her friends take shelter in an abandoned uranium mine. Over the next few days, Zoe's hearing sharpens drastically, beyond what any normal human being can detect. She tells her friends, only to learn that four others have an increased sense as well. Only Kieran, the new boy from Scotland, isn't affected.

Fashioning themselves into superheroes, the group tries to stop the strange occurrences happening in their little town. Muggings, break-ins, disappearances, and murder begin to hit too close to home. It leads the team to think someone knows about their secret - someone who wants them all dead.

An incredulous group of heroes. A traitor in the midst. Some dreams are written in blood.

Courage Runs Red
The Blood Red Series
Book 1 is FREE

WHAT IF COURAGE WAS your only option?

When Kallie lands a college interview with the city's new hot-shot police officer, she has no idea everything in her life is about to change. The detective is young, handsome and seems to have an unnatural ability to stop the increasing local crime rate. Detective Liam's particular interest in Kallie sends her heart and head stumbling over each other.

When a raging blood feud between vampires spills into her home, Kallie gets caught in the middle. Torn between love and family loyalty she must find the courage to fight what she fears the most and possibly risk everything, even if it means dying for those she loves.

Daughter of Darkness - Victoria
Only Death Could Stop Her Now
The Daughters of Darkness is a series of female heroines who may or
may not know each other, but all have the same father, Vlad Montour.
Victoria is a Hunter Vampire

Paranormal
HUNTRESS SERIES
USA TODAY BESTSELLING AUTHOR
W.J. MAY
LOOK BACK
MASTER
PERMISSION

PROPHECY SERIES
USA TODAY BESTSELLING AUTHOR
W.J. MAY
PROPHECY
PROPHECY
PROPHECY
W.J. MAY
W.J. MAY
W.J. MAY

Don't miss out!

Visit the website below and you can sign up to receive emails whenever W.J. May publishes a new book. There's no charge and no obligation.

https://books2read.com/r/B-A-SSF-JPVIB

BOOKS 2 READ

Connecting independent readers to independent writers.

Did you love *Converted*? Then you should read *Paranormal Huntress BOX SET*[1] by W.J. May!

USA Today Bestselling author, W.J. May, brings you to a new level of fantasy. Fans of Underworld and paranormal worlds will love this story!

PARANORMAL HUNTRESS BOX SET is the first 3 books of the Paranormal Huntress series - altogether in one collection!

"The wise learn many things from their enemies."

My name's Atlanta Skolar, and I'm a huntress. No, not the vampire-slaying type, or the ever-brooding Winchester brothers from *Supernatural*. I live a relatively normal life—during the day at least. I go to school, have friends, and try my best to survive Uncle James' horrendous cooking.

---

1. https://books2read.com/u/3J8kGv

2. https://books2read.com/u/3J8kGv

However, the nights in the city of Calen are not always calm. There's a thin veil between our world and the world of monsters, the good and the bad. I'm one of the few who stands between the two. With the help of my uncle, who's taken me in since my parents' deaths, I spend the nights making sure the balance is maintained and that each side keeps to their respective places.

At least, that was until something rattled the cages and everything hit the fan. There's a new evil in town, an evil that's been here before, and it may be responsible for my parents' deaths. An evil that isn't satisfied with the balance. It'll do all it can to make sure darkness falls over Calen and the rest of the world once again.

Scary? That ain't the half of it.

It's particularly interested in me.

Why? No idea.

But it's my job as a huntress to make sure the evil is stopped, no matter what.

BOOK 2

The city of Calen has fallen.

The forces that once held the city as one are scattered and drained of power. Adelaide, one of the witches who's haunted and threatened the peace once made by the elders in the territory, has regained her power by releasing the hybrids she's created. She's determined to destroy Calen and all those who stand in her way.

Atlanta, the Druid huntress, responsible for unlocking the hybrids and the murder of her uncle, tries to come to terms with what's happened.

The fate of Calen rests in too few hands. Divided sanctions, Vamps, Wolf and Druid, must unify or each race stands no chance of survival.

BOOK 3

Calen has fallen. Everlore has fallen. Atlanta Skolar is on the run. Barely escaping the clutches of Adelaide, and believing her mother is dead, she escapes the fires of the ancient city.

Her escape, though, is bittersweet. Coupled with the unknown ability she has recently discovered, and the curious case of her platinum colored hair, she has yet to find a way to defeat the witch and her followers. Joined by her band of trusted friends, Atlanta must work to find the remaining Lunar Books and figure out the secrets within if she wants to stop Adelaide's conquest for complete dominance.

But with hybrids and the compelled hot on her trail, the task seems almost impossible. Atlanta must find the strength within her, and unleash the powers of the Coven Master, if she wants to ensure the survival of her friends...and herself.

SERIES:
Never Look Back
Coven Master
Alpha's Permission
Blood Bonding
Oracle of Nightmares
Shadows in the Night
Read more at www.wjmaybooks.com.

Also by W.J. May

Bit-Lit Series
Lost Vampire
Cost of Blood
Price of Death

Blood Red Series
Courage Runs Red
The Night Watch
Marked by Courage
Forever Night
The Other Side of Fear
Blood Red Box Set Books #1-5

Daughters of Darkness: Victoria's Journey
Victoria
Huntress
Coveted (A Vampire & Paranormal Romance)
Twisted
Daughter of Darkness - Victoria - Box Set

Great Temptation Series
The Devil's Footsteps
Heaven's Command
Mortals Surrender

Hidden Secrets Saga
Seventh Mark - Part 1
Seventh Mark - Part 2
Marked By Destiny
Compelled
Fate's Intervention
Chosen Three
The Hidden Secrets Saga: The Complete Series

Kerrigan Chronicles
Stopping Time
A Passage of Time
Ticking Clock
Secrets in Time
Time in the City
Ultimate Future

Mending Magic Series
Lost Souls
Illusion of Power
Challenging the Dark

Castle of Power
Limits of Magic
Protectors of Light

Omega Queen Series
Discipline
Bravery
Courage
Conquer
Strength
Validation

Paranormal Huntress Series
Never Look Back
Coven Master
Alpha's Permission
Blood Bonding
Oracle of Nightmares
Shadows in the Night
Paranormal Huntress BOX SET

Prophecy Series
Only the Beginning
White Winter
Secrets of Destiny

Revamped Series
Hidden
Banished
Converted

Royal Factions
The Price For Peace
The Cost for Surviving
The Punishment For Deception

The Chronicles of Kerrigan
Rae of Hope
Dark Nebula
House of Cards
Royal Tea
Under Fire
End in Sight
Hidden Darkness
Twisted Together
Mark of Fate
Strength & Power
Last One Standing
Rae of Light
The Chronicles of Kerrigan Box Set Books # 1 - 6

The Chronicles of Kerrigan: Gabriel

Living in the Past
Present For Today
Staring at the Future

The Chronicles of Kerrigan Prequel
Christmas Before the Magic
Question the Darkness
Into the Darkness
Fight the Darkness
Alone in the Darkness
Lost in Darkness
The Chronicles of Kerrigan Prequel Series Books #1-3

The Chronicles of Kerrigan Sequel
A Matter of Time
Time Piece
Second Chance
Glitch in Time
Our Time
Precious Time

The Hidden Secrets Saga
Seventh Mark (part 1 & 2)

The Kerrigan Kids
School of Potential

Myths & Magic
Kith & Kin
Playing With Power
Line of Ancestry
Descent of Hope
Illusion of Shadows

The Queen's Alpha Series
Eternal
Everlasting
Unceasing
Evermore
Forever
Boundless
Prophecy
Protected
Foretelling
Revelation
Betrayal
Resolved
The Queen's Alpha Box Set

The Senseless Series
Radium Halos - Part 1
Radium Halos - Part 2
Nonsense
Perception
The Senseless - Box Set Books #1-4

Standalone
Shadow of Doubt (Part 1 & 2)
Five Shades of Fantasy
Zwarte Nevel
Shadow of Doubt - Part 1
Shadow of Doubt - Part 2
Four and a Half Shades of Fantasy
Dream Fighter
What Creeps in the Night
Forest of the Forbidden
Arcane Forest: A Fantasy Anthology
The First Fantasy Box Set

Watch for more at www.wjmaybooks.com.

About the Author

About W.J. May

Welcome to USA TODAY BESTSELLING author W.J. May's Page! SIGN UP for W.J. May's Newsletter to find out about new releases, updates, cover reveals and even freebies! http://eepurl.com/97aYf

Website: http://www.wjmaybooks.com

Facebook: http://www.facebook.com/pages/Author-WJ-May-FAN-PAGE/141170442608149?ref=hl *Please feel free to connect with me and share your comments. I love connecting with my readers.* W.J. May grew up in the fruit belt of Ontario. Crazy-happy childhood, she always has had a vivid imagination and loads of energy. After her father passed away in 2008, from a six-year battle with cancer (which she still believes he won the fight against), she began to write again. A passion she'd loved for years, but realized life was too short to keep putting it off. She is a writer of Young Adult, Fantasy Fiction and where ever else her little muses take her.

Read more at www.wjmaybooks.com.

La cruz marcó su vida,

el dolor su camino guió,

sin motivo la acusan,

de algo que no hizo,

solo lucha por vivir,

solo lucha por reponerse,

reponerse contra un castigo,

que le ha tocado

sin merecerse.